AND A BUTTERFLY SOARED

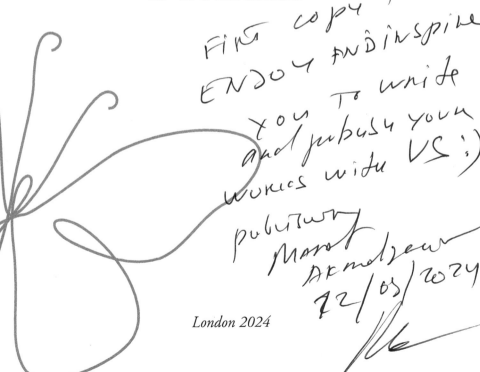

First copy to
Enjoy and inspire
you to write
and publish your
works with VS :)

publishing

Maros
Akmoldzew
12/05/2024

London 2024

Published by Hertfordshire Press Ltd © 2024
e-mail: publisher@hertfordshirepress.com
www.hertfordshirepress.com

Hertfordshire Press Award
from Eurasian Creative Guild (London)

AND A BUTTERFLY SOARED

Lusine Aleksanyan ©

Edited by Jonathan Campion
Design by Alexandra Rey
Cover illustration by Razmik Ohanyan

British Library Catalogue in Publication Data
A catalogue record for this book is available from the British Library
Library of Congress in Publication Data
A catalogue record for this book has been requested

ISBN: 978-1-913356-82-8

CONTENTS

THE GIRL
WHO SINGS

Prologue

2014. Early September

Dreams are the royal road to the unconscious.
— Sigmund Freud

She stood at the entrance to the long corridor, hesitant to step forward. She didn't know what lay ahead, but the darkness that surrounded her on all sides made it clear that she could delay no longer. She had to move forward. After taking a few steps, she noticed that at the end of the corridor there were two paths, one to the left and one to the right. She didn't know which way to go. The inner voice was silent. She turned left. With each step, the corridor became narrower and narrower. She quickened her pace, afraid of being crushed by the huge walls that rose on either side. Quick steps that turned into a sprint led down the tangled corridors. She felt trapped.

Realising she was in a maze, she tried to turn back, but it was no use. The corridors had narrowed so much that she could barely move. Her breathing accelerated. She'd never noticed any signs of claustrophobia before. And at this moment, the lack of space and air had her on the verge of fainting. Cold sweat and shivers ran through her body. Her heart was racing. She was ready to give up, to plunge into the abyss of nothingness, to surrender to death, when suddenly a white light descended from somewhere above, its radiance and unknown power beginning to push the walls back and give the helpless girl a new breath.

Milena woke up drenched in sweat. She brushed away the damp hair that clung to the back of her head and forehead. She breathed frequently, in rhythm with her heartbeat. The sensations of sleep were so obvious that she half sat up in her bed and looked around to see where she was. Instinctively, she switched on the night light on the bedside table. The watch she'd taken off before going to bed showed five in the morning. "Another two hours," Milena thought. She went back to bed and wrapped herself in a blanket. The sleep was gone. She was afraid to close her eyes for fear of the narrow maze. She tossed and turned in bed, replaying her latest nightmare in her mind, trying to make sense of it. Something inside told her it wasn't good. But the light that appeared out of nowhere gave Milena hope that whatever had happened would be all right.

She didn't notice that a few minutes later she fell into a deep, dreamless sleep that lasted until morning. And the night light was still on.

The past had been on Milena's mind a lot lately. It gave her no peace. The first stage, the first competition, the first concert. It was like yesterday. But it was already eighteen years ago.

She's five years old. A kindergarten graduation matinee. Because of her good voice and her beautiful face, little golden–haired Milena got the role of Cinderella in the play. As beautiful dresses for girls were rare in those years, Milena's mother had to find a rich golden dress from an acquaintance. White sandals, and white socks with lace, that, to Milena's great regret, were only just visible under the long dress. It was the first time she had worn them. A small stone crown adorned her luxuriant golden curls. Milena's eyes lit up with happiness as she looked at herself in the mirror after a quick cooking session.

At twenty–three, Milena had already forgotten the last time she had been so happy over something so small.

It was the day she sang for the first time on the small stage of the kindergarten hall, which had seemed huge to her at the time. Milena remembered that day for a long time. Forever.

First class. First lesson at school. First music lesson. First steps. First disappointments. First victory.

Milena grew up. School subjects became more difficult, exams more important, concerts more responsible. It was time to choose a subject, a teacher and a university. Although music came first for Milena, she was well aware that it did not have the full future she wanted. How she chose medical school, especially dentistry, she did not understand. But already from the first classes for admission she realised that she had made the right choice. And having entered, and being a student of a medical university, she realised the correctness of her choice. Her two specialities were closely related. They complemented each other, making the golden–haired girl's life full. Milena devoted a decent amount of time to both, managing to be the best in both spheres.

– Milena, you were always first. In everything. You're smart, beautiful, talented, kind. You have opened many doors, but you have so many more to go through, so many more doors to open and so many more to close. You have a whole life ahead of you, full of all the most interesting and beautiful things. There will also be difficulties and disappointments. But you have to take it all for granted, overcome it, and keep on living. You will succeed. Because it can't be any other way.

Every time Milena faced an obstacle, every time she lost her strength and put her hands down, her mother knew how to lift her up, how to help her. And she always succeeded.

Over the years, thanks to her mother's advice, Milena has learned to fight for her goals and desires. She learned to love, to admire, to appreciate, to cherish and, whatever it was, to go through life with her head held high.

Chapter 1

2014. The end of September

Friendship is settling for the possible, without demanding the proper.
— *Aristotle*

– Hello darling. How is my inimitable friend? – Astine's voice always sounded cheerful and had a positive effect on Milena, no matter what mood she was in.

– Hello, Astine. Everything is fine. I'm going to the shopping centre with my mother, – Milena said.

– Oh, that's great. Hi to mum.

– Hi, Astine. How are you? – Sveta replied.

– Hello, Sveta. Fine. Milena, I'm going to kill you. Didn't you tell me you had the loudspeaker on? It's a good thing I didn't say too much.

– Astine, you know I never answer for myself when I'm driving.

– Do you young ladies have any secrets from me?

– No, Mum.

– No, Sveta. No, you don't.

Sveta just laughed. She was always friendly with her friends and the children's friends. And she was always welcomed like a member of the family.

– Milena, are you free tonight?

Milena looked at Sveta before she answered. She nodded in agreement.

– Yes, Astine. Why? Any plans?

– No, nothing specific, to be honest, but I'd like to see you. I've already called Ani. She's up for it. Armen is out of town, my parents are going to a friend's for dinner and I'm all alone.

– Oh, my darling. We won't leave you alone. Be prepared. Mum and I are just going to do a bit of shopping and then I'll take them home and pick you up.

– Love you. See you soon. Bye, Sveta. Kisses.

– Bye, darling.

Milena and Astine had known each other since secondary school. They had been in the same class for three years, and when they started medical school they were in the same group. They were family friends and inseparable. A girl of medium height, medium build, with long straight ash–coloured hair and grey eyes was very similar to Milena. Many people thought they were sisters. They were sisters. Different blood types and surnames did not change their inseparable relationship.

The girls met Ani in their third year when she joined their group. A beautiful tall girl with green eyes and dark brown hair, the friends found a common language within a few days and accepted her into their small, friendly world.

The three of them appeared together everywhere. Before, during and after school they were together. At all parties and events, the trio could not be seen apart. The iron chains of friendship bound them together forever.

– What did you buy? – asked Astine before she could get into Milena's black BMW.

– Yes, nothing much. A few t–shirts for me and a dress for

Mum. What's new?

– The same old stuff. This is the second day I haven't seen my beloved. It's turning my head. I miss him terribly.

– Has something happened? – asked Milena, keeping her eyes on the road.

– Yes… no… Friday night he went to Ijevan with his father on some business. I don't know when he'll be back. So I'm suffering here without him.

– Oh, you poor thing. Doesn't even our company cheer you up and make you happy?

– Of course it does. You're my very best. Especially you. And you know it, – said Astine, – looking lovingly at her friend.

– Of course I do. And you are for me. – Milena turned her head to her friend and looked at her with the same tenderness.

– You'd better watch the road, – Astine said suddenly.

– And you don't distract me.

– If you say so.

They never spoke another word on the road.

– I love this café. The coffee here is incredible. – Before she crossed the threshold, Ani continued to praise her choice of small, cosy café on Abovyan Street.

– Is there at least one thing here that you do not care about?

– I couldn't stand another compliment from my friend, – Ani said to Astine.

Ani paused for a moment, looked around attentively and then replied.

– No.

– That's fine. Now please be nice and change the subject.

– Okay, said a slightly offended Ani.

– What's wrong with you? – said Astine, turning sharply to Milena.

– I'm fine, – Milena replied, surprised.

– Yes, what is it?

– Astine, it's really OK.

– Why don't I believe it?

– That's your problem, – Milena said, looking at her friend.

– Are you kidding me? – Astine didn't give up yet.

Milena didn't answer. Her look was enough for Astine to understand her friend's answer. There was a heavy silence. Each of them stared at her own plate of dessert, which neither of them dared to touch.

– I'm sorry, Astine, – Milena said, putting down her clean fork.

– For what? – Astine couldn't hide her surprise.

Ani just remained silent and watched her unpredictable friends. Ani was often silent during their arguments and reconciliations, because it happened too often. Unable to anticipate her friends' moods or prevent another fight, she preferred to spend those moments in silence until the passions finally subsided.

– Forgive me for always contradicting you.

– Milena, don't. You don't have to answer me. It's just that I can see that something is wrong with you. You're not yourself. And that's why I want to do something to help you. At least find out what's on your mind. I want to hear you out.

– I know you do. I'm sorry. You wanted what was best for you, and I...

– Milena, please. Just talk to us. What's wrong?

Astine looked at Ani intently, looking for support. Ani, to Astine's surprise, immediately understood her friend's hint.

– Milena, you know you can always rely on us. We will always listen and support you. In every situation, – Ani began in a soft, calm voice.

– Jesus, – Milena said suddenly, lowering her head.

– What, Milena? – Ani was frightened.

– How stupid I am. How stupid! – Milena repeated without raising her head.

– What's going on? Will you tell me? – Astine got angry.

– I'm sad. Terribly. Sometimes I manage to hide my true feelings, but sometimes I can't. I miss Aren. – At the mention of her brother's name, the first tear rolled down Milena's cheek. – I miss him terribly. I find it hard to breathe. I wake up in the morning, go into his room, see his untouched, unmade bed, and a lump rises in my throat and chokes me. I can't deal with it. I can't share it with my parents, because I know it's not easy for them either.

– Milena, my love, I know how hard this is for you. We all miss Aren. But the thought that he is alive and well, serving his country, albeit far from home, should give you hope and patience.

Astine spoke quietly, stroking her friend's arm.

Ani was unable to speak or support her friend. The same lump in her throat had been there for months. A lump that no one knew about. Not even those closest to her.

It had only been four months since Aren had been in the army, and she still couldn't get used to his absence. He'd left at the end of June after completing his undergraduate studies at medical school. They went to school together from the first grade, graduated together, studied together for admission and then enrolled together, but at different faculties: she at the Faculty of Dentistry and he at the Faculty of General Medicine.

They were inseparable, although they were completely different in character and appearance. The only thing they had in common was their tall stature and very different beauty. Unlike his sister, Aren was a fair–skinned, green–eyed blonde. But when they were together, no one could pass them without being noticed. They were like two gods descending from Mount Olympus.

– Yes, I know. But I can't help feeling empty for a minute.

– Oh, darling. You mustn't torture yourself like this. If you go on like this, there won't be anything left of you in two years when Aren comes. And he won't like that. He probably wants to see a healthy, beautiful and happy little sister when he comes home, not a half–dead medical graduate. So pull yourself together. Stop torturing yourself. At least for his sake.

Astine took a full glass of chilled black tea and drank every last drop. Ani followed her friend's example, but could only take a sip.

– Yes, Astine, you're right. I must be strong. For him, for my parents. I have to.

Milena looked at her friends with tear–filled eyes.

– But, damn it, it's so hard. – Milena couldn't hold back her emotions. Tears rolled one after another.

– Come on, my girl. Calm down. You can't do that.

Astine, stretching a little from her seat, hugged her friend tightly. Ani, sensitised by the whole picture and the emotions that filled her soul, also gave vent to tears.

– I can imagine what the people from the neighbouring tables think of us, – said Astine, continuing to hug her friend.

– Me too, – said Milena, laughing slightly through her tears.

Ani also smiled slightly. And then the laughter came as suddenly as the recent tears.

– All right, settle down. They'll take us straight to the nuthouse.

Astine finally released Milena from her embrace.

– I know what you need. – Astine said, while her friends were wiping away the last tears with paper towels.

– And what is it? – Milena asked.

– You need a boyfriend, – replied Astine without much doubt.

– A boyfriend? – the surprised Ani and Milena asked together.

– Yes. Why are you so surprised? Did you, Milena, react like that to the word boyfriend? Did you change your orientation?

– Idiot.

– Am I the stupid one? I have a normal life. With a normal guy. I don't know who you're waiting for. Especially you, Astine said to Milena, you have so many admirers and you're still alone. If you had a private life, you wouldn't dwell on your brother's service, you'd take it for granted. No, Milena, you must have a life. You need it. You need love. Real love. The kind that makes your head spin and lifts you up to the sky, that makes you forget everything and plunge into the abyss of happiness.

Milena listened to her friend with unwavering disbelief. Noticing this, she continued.

– Believe me, Milena. Love is strong. It can do anything. It can make something out of nothing. And you need it. Trust me.

– Yes, Astine, I do. But how do I find her? I don't like anyone. And I've given up hope that I ever will.

– Cut the crap. Of course, you will. Soon. My heart feels that your life is about to change.

– Oh, you're my Astine. I love you. I hope so. Time will tell. All in good time.

All in good time. Time will tell. There's no hurry. We must be patient.

At first glance, these seem like simple, easy–to–say sentences. But it takes so much strength and will to make even one of them a reality.

Chapter 2

2014. Mid–October

Birth is that portion of immortality
and eternity that is given to a mortal being.
— Plato

Milena had been awake all night. When she heard the song "My heart will go on" by Celine Dion, she realised that it was seven in the morning and it was time to get up. Milena switched off the alarm clock, got out of her warm, inviting bed and went to the window. The sun had long since awakened, welcoming all living and non–living things with its warm embrace. As she opened the window, Milena felt a cool breeze blowing in. Goosebumps ran down her body. She took her time closing the window and went to prepare for the day that her deepest hopes and dreams were connected.

While Milena was applying make–up to her beautiful golden complexion, her parents approached, holding some kind of package in their hands. Milena got up from her chair and walked over to them. The three of them exchanged tight hugs and kisses.

– Happy birthday, darling, said Sveta, a tall, beautiful, well–groomed woman of about forty–five.

– Happy birthday, my daughter.

Milena's father, Oleg, was also distinguished by his youth,

beauty and virility. His very appearance exuded reliability and security.

– Thank you, Mum, Dad. I love you very much.

– We love you too, Milena, – Sveta said, hugging her daughter again. 'And we have a little present for you.'

Milena was always surprised by the word "little" because every year it was a car, a new musical instrument or a European holiday. This year she didn't know what to expect from her parents.

Sveta handed her daughter a small golden package. Gently, Maria accepted the gift and began to unwrap it. Inside was a gold chain with an oval gold pendant set with emerald or, as it is sometimes called, green ice, a stone that symbolises purity and faithfulness. The Greeks called it 'the stone of radiance', and in Russia the emerald was considered a stone of wisdom, equanimity and hope.

Milena opened the pendant and saw two pictures on either side. One was of her parents, the other of her and her twin brother. Milena could not believe her eyes and threw herself around her parents' necks.

– Thank you, thank you. This is the best present I've ever been given in my life.

She couldn't hold back her tears, which reflected happiness, longing and pain. Her parents were as excited as she was.

– I miss him so much, – Milena said through her tears.

– We miss him too, – her tearful parents agreed.

– So, on your birthday we will make a gift to our family and today at noon we will go to him at the station, – said Oleg, looking at his daughter's face.

– Oh my God. Really? I'm so happy, I'm so happy! It will be the best birthday.

Milena's eyes sparkled.

– So, I'll go to the hospital for a little while for my lesson, then I'll take my leave and come quickly. Okay? – said Milena excitedly.

– Yes, but be careful, don't step on the gas, – said the father as he left his daughter's room.

– Your father and I will not go to work today, so that we have time to get ready to leave. You go to class in peace, I'll take care of everything.

Milena's parents had their own law firm, so they never had a problem with skipping work.

– Yes, by the way, the dress is very suitable, – Sveta said, and, kissing her daughter again, left the room, closing the door quietly behind her.

A tight dress of emerald colour above the knees with long sleeves was decorated with a new pendant, which complemented Milena's image. Sitting down in front of the mirror, she looked at her beautiful reflection. In it she saw what she had missed. Her eyes were burning again. Burning with the fire of happiness and hope.

It was nine in the morning when Milena drove up to "Muratsan" Hospital Complex in her black BMW x5, looking for a parking space. Stopping the car, she took quick steps, as fast as her high heels would allow her, towards the lift. Before she reached the last one, she noticed a tall girl with long blue–black hair who was most likely waiting for the lift. Milena immediately recognised the girl as her classmate Maria, who also happened to have a birthday that day.

Milena approached her classmate, greeted her, congratulated her and received congratulations in return. Although they were classmates and Facebook friends, they had never met. When the lift doors opened, they entered together. In the few seconds it took to get to the fifth floor, Milena caught a glimpse of Maria, who looked so much like Snow White. And as their gazes locked for a moment, Milena caught a glimpse of sparks in Maria's coal–black eyes, which could tell her classmate's state of mind at that moment. When the lift doors opened, the girls stepped out, smiled at each other and, having missed each other, each of them headed towards their classroom

Milena entered the small classroom and, after apologising to the teacher for being a little late, went to her seat, quickly changed into her scrubs and sat down next to Astine. Her classmates, whoever had made it, whispered congratulations to Milena. And the paediatrics teacher, as if oblivious, went on talking about the peculiarities of child development.

At half past eleven, during the break, Milena explained the situation to the teacher and asked him to let her go early. Strangely enough, he agreed without hesitation. During the fifteen–minute break, Milena had time to receive congratulations and good wishes from her favourite classmates.

– Astine, Ani, I have to leave in an hour. We're going to Aren with my parents today. Can you believe it? I can't believe I'm going to see him soon.

Milena saw the way Ani's eyes sparkled at her words.

– No, don't get me wrong, it's wonderful that you're going to your brother's, especially on his birthday, but I'm terribly sorry we won't be spending the day together.

– Me too, – Ani said, her eyes downcast.

– Yeah, I wish we could all be together today, but I can't give up the trip to the Aren. Listen, – said Milena with a special joy, – let's go together.

Her friends looked at her perplexed.

– With you to Karabakh, to Aren? – asked surprised and no

less excited Ani.

– Well, yes. – Milena answered, pleased with her idea.

– I have to talk to Armen, – said Astine, quickly dialling her boyfriend's number.

Ani and Milena waited impatiently for Armen's answer. Astine stepped back to talk, but her friends couldn't stop watching the expression on her face. When Astine approached them again, all radiant, they realised without words Armen's positive answer. Ani, who was also eager to go with everyone, called her parents and somehow managed to persuade them to go.

At noon Milena and her parents, Armen, Astine and Ani went to Aren's house in Nagorno–Karabakh.

There was no better birthday in the life of the twins, who after a short but lingering and difficult separation spent an unforgettable day in the circle of family and friends, in the circle of the closest and most sincere people.

Chapter 3

2014. Mid–November

Love is the great madness Of man and woman.
— Paulo Coelho

The car stopped not far from the club, which was crowded with young people. Milena tried to strain her eyesight and see at least one familiar person among the crowd, but she could not manage it. Giving up, she took her phone out of her purse and, unlocking it, went through the list of recent calls. Selecting Astine's number, she pressed the call button. It buzzed. No one answered. Milena had already moved the phone away from her ear when she heard her friend's voice from afar.

– Hello, hello, Milena, hello.....

Milena realised that her friend was trying to shout over the music, but the music was so loud that Astine couldn't manage it at all.

– Astine, I'm already at the entrance, – Milena said calmly, not hoping that her friend would hear her.

– Milena, I can't hear you, wait a minute, I'll come out and call you back, she kept shouting to Astine.

– Milena said, but her friend could hardly hear her this time.

Before answering, Milena looked towards the entrance and saw her friend squeezing through the crowd and onto the pavement.

– Yes, Astine, I saw you, wait, I'll be right there.

– All right.

Milena saw her friend turn off her phone and looked around. Milena paid the taxi driver, got out and walked towards her friend. Astine saw her and came over.

– Hi, said Milena.

– Hi, darling, – said Astine.

The friends hugged each other, even though they had only seen each other a few hours earlier.

– Did a lot of people come? – Milena asked.

– No. Just me and Armen. And we've only just arrived. We wanted to wait for you at the entrance, but we decided to come in and make the last preparations before the boys arrived.

– We did the right thing. Don't just stand there, – said Milena, pointing to the crowd of young people who refused to leave.

– She's with us, – Astine said to the tall guard in black who was covering the entrance with all his height and body. Strangely, he smiled and moved away from the door, allowing Milena and Astine to pass.

From the threshold, the sounds of Eminem and Kanye West's song "Monster" reached Milena. After passing through the corridor, whose walls and ceiling were covered with mirrors, Astine struggled to open the huge door at the end of the corridor. A song filled the room.

– Damn door, – Astine snorted.

After letting Milena pass, Astine let go of the door. Once inside, Milena stood hesitantly. The music and atmosphere that filled her soul in a matter of seconds was mesmerising and kept her from moving. The source of the little light in the dark room were small disco lights.

– Milena, are you coming? – asked Astine, who was already on her way to Armen.

– Yes, of course. I'm coming, – Milena replied and followed her friend.

They walked along the tables to the end where their seats were and where Armen was standing.

– Hi, Armen. Happy holidays, – said Milena and hugged her friend's boyfriend.

– Thank you, Milena, – said Armen, also hugging Milena. – You look beautiful. Did you try it on for me?

– Of course, for you, – said Milena, laughing.

– Why are you standing there? Sit down. The others won't be joining us any time soon.

The tables had already been moved and the chairs arranged. The waitress, a girl of about twenty–five, with long black hair tied back in a ponytail, wearing white shirt and classic black trousers, was arranging the cutlery with particular elegance. Armen stared at the waitress, which earned him a kick in the shins from Astine.

– Ouch, – Armen said with a displeased look on his face.

– Yes, darling? Is something wrong? – Astine asked with a grin, as if nothing had happened.

– No, darling, everything is fine, – Armen said.

Milena, who had witnessed the couple's little showdown, couldn't help smiling. She caught her friend's eye and winked in support. Astine smiled and winked back. The screen of Armen's phone lit up, but there was no ringtone.

– Yes, hello. Where are you? Can't get in? You said you were at an event? What event? Wait, I'll be right out, – Armen got up from his seat. – I'll be right out, – heading towards the exit.

She nodded without answering. Milena had always admired

her friend's character. She always knew where and how to behave with Armen. His character was no gift and everyone knew it, but Astine always managed to cope with him. Thanks to her, he changed in front of her eyes, in a good way, of course. There were still some flaws, but Milena was 100% sure that her friend would soon get over them.

Armen and Astine met in the cafeteria, standing in line. Armen noticed Astine standing in front of him, and from that moment on she never left his sight. During the fifteen minutes that Milena and Astine stood in the queue, Armen did his best to get Astine's attention. And he had succeeded. Milena had always admired Armen's persistence in winning the young beauty's unyielding heart.

At the time, Astine was finishing her bachelor's degree at the Faculty of Dentistry and Armen was finishing his degree at the Faculty of General Medicine. And for a year and a half they were inseparable.

Milena and Astine had barely exchanged a few words when they noticed some boys coming towards them.

– Hi, Astine. You look beautiful, said a tall, handsome guy, hugging and kissing Astine.

– Hi, Gor. Thank you, she said with a smile.

Milena didn't recognise Gor. While she was looking at the stranger, Armen's classmate Anna and her boyfriend Mukuch, whom Milena had known for a long time and with whom she was quite friendly, came over to say hello.

– Gor, you must have already met Anna and Mukuch? – Astine turned to Gor.

– Of course, my dear, I introduced them at the entrance, – Armen interrupted without letting Gor answer.

– Well, Gor, come on, I'll introduce you to my close friend, –

Astine took Gor by the hand and led him over to Milena, – this is Milena, beautiful, intelligent, simply a miracle, and of course my close friend.

– Astine, come on, – Milena said sheepishly.

– What's true is true, – said Milena.

– Milena, this is Gor, a close friend of Armen's. He came back this summer from Moscow, where he finished his medical studies. By the way, Gor is already a resident traumatologist at the First University Hospital.

– Nice to meet you, – Milena and Gor smiled at the same time. Milena smiled with her usual embarrassment and Gor smiled with confidence.

When he held out his hand, she did not hesitate to shake it. Her delicate hand sank into his strong, firm, large hand. A current ran through Milena's body as soon as he touched her. There was no way she could let go of his hand. Invisible chains seemed to bind their hands together, preventing them from separating. Her strange behaviour could not go unnoticed.

– Oh, Milena, look, Ani is here too, – Astine broke the uncomfortable silence and pointed to the entrance.

She took Milena's free hand and pulled her towards her. Milena, seemingly coming to her senses from her hypnotised state, let go of the hand holding Horus's arm and followed her friend. They made their way to the exit, where Ani came towards them, smiling.

– Yes, what's wrong with you, Milena? – asked Astine in a whisper.

– I don't know, – Milena replied in shock.

– I think I know, – Astine muttered.

Milena had no time to contradict her friend, for Ani was approaching them.

– Hello, my darlings. My sweet ones. How I missed you, – Ani said, hugging her friends tightly.

– Ani, we've only seen each other recently, – said Astine.

– You're a bad girl, Astine. You could have reciprocated, – said Ani, jokingly insulting. – Milena, what's the matter with you? Are you so confused or frightened with joy? What's that look on your face?

– Don't ask, – Astine said, looking at Ani meaningfully.

– Armen, darling, congratulations.

Ani hugged and kissed Armen as he came towards them.

– Thank you, Ani. Why are you standing there? Come to our tables, – Armen said, giving way for the three friends.

Milena followed with her head bowed. The trembling did not stop. Something strange and unfamiliar was awakening in her. She felt the approach of danger and happiness, something she would have to experience for the first time in her life. Something she was not at all prepared for.

Milena sat down at the end table, next to her sat Ani, and across from her sat a young couple, Anna and Mukuch, and Armen's brother Albert. Not far from Milena were Astine and Armen, Gor and the newcomers Karine, Mara, Stepan and Petros, who were also classmates and good friends of Armen.

A familiar waitress filled the girls' glasses with scarlet wine, while the boys downed their first crystal shot of vodka. Neighbouring tables were already occupied. The music was playing. The dance floor was filling up. The evening promised to be hot.

Milena couldn't see Gor because he was sitting in her direction, three people away from her. Only occasionally saw his hands, each time she got goose bumps. Breathing became difficult, almost impossible. She was afraid of this state. Scared of what she didn't understand. And what she didn't understand was how a handshake, a look of black eyes could put her in such a state. After all, they had only just met, had only spoken two words. Just two words: "Nice to meet you." Two words, two hands and a pair of black eyes that had turned her whole inner world upside down.

The club, alcohol, congratulations, friends, music. Astine and Armen, embraced, circled the dance floor. Milena, admiringly, watched them. A beautiful couple, true love.

Mukuch, who sat next to her and hugged her, pulled Anna by the arm, inviting her to dance. Ani was taken by Albert. The others also went to dance. The dance floor captivated Milena. The song possessed her, taking her in its chains. Mesmerised by the song and the atmosphere, Milena suddenly felt a warm breath in her ear. A shiver ran through her whole body and she froze.

– Shall we dance? – she heard.

Without answering anything, she obeyed peacefully without even turning around. She recognised the "master" of those two words perfectly. He was leading her forward. Only forward, towards the dance floor. Taking her wrist sharply and with some roughness, he turned her to face him. Her eyes sparkled, but there was a sense of fright and confusion in them. She could not move. The music, his hands, the music, his gaze, the music, the movement. He placed his hands on her hips without even asking permission, and she didn't even pull away. He took the first steps, setting the mechanism in motion. She loosened up. Her muscles relaxed. The body became as light as a feather. Moving to the rhythm of the music. They were very close. She could smell the scent of his perfume that drove her mad. She was completely at his mercy, the prisoner of a stranger to whom she had opened herself too soon.

"Milena, come to your senses, please. Come to your senses

before someone notices. Come to your senses before he drives you completely mad," the inner voice said. "Don't care about anyone. What do you care about them? Seize the moment. Enjoy the music, this guy, these minutes. No one has the right to judge you," the other voice urged. The two voices argued in her pretty head. But the second voice won. Its conviction prevailed. What had she done wrong? It was just a dance. Just a dance.

The song "Like A G6" was replaced by a club remix of Nelly's "Just A Dream". Milena didn't notice the change in the music, she only felt the change in Gor's movements. Snippets of the song came to her ears. But at that moment she didn't care what was playing. What mattered was that it was playing, and playing continuously.

Midnight. The evening was coming to an end. The guests were already leaving. Cinderella's time was running out. The magic was dissolving. Disappeared.

Armen saw the guests off one by one. Astine, Milena and Ani were still sitting at the table when Armen approached them with Gor.

– Well, one last toast and then we'll go home, – Armen said, raising his glass.

The glasses and shot glasses were filled.

– Let's drink to a successful evening and another unforgettable day in our lives, – said Armen, smiling at his friends.

– Hurrah, – the guys shouted at once, draining their glasses.

The smile never left Milena's face. Her eyes sparkled. She was happy. What exactly caused this change in her, she didn't understand yet. But she realised that this evening had given her not only another memory, but also the thing she wanted most in her heart.

Chapter 4

2014. End of November

If you want to touch a rose, don't be afraid to cut your hands,
If you want to drink, don't be afraid to get a hangover.
And if you want a love that's beautiful, reverent and passionate.
If you want to burn your heart in vain, don't be afraid!
— *Omar Khayyam*

The day after her birthday, Milena went to her Facebook page and was delighted to find a message from Gor Aznavuryan asking her to add him as a friend. After she accepted, they began an active virtual communication. Each day began with the word "hello", followed by endless discussions on all sorts of topics, and in the evening, she would say "good night" and slip into the abyss of dreams with an unmistakable smile on her face.

Those around her noticed a visible change in her. After her brother left, she rarely smiled; there was always a sadness in her eyes. But what was happening to her lately could only be described by one word – happiness.

She could not hold back her smile, could not hold back the accumulation of positive emotions. Falling in love had given her wings that taught her to fly without falling to the ground. Her eyes sparkled, the blush never left her delicate face.

Even the way she dressed was different. There was a special elegance to every outfit she wore. Her hair was always beautifully styled and shimmered like a cover, even in bad weather.

Her smartphone was not just in her hand when she slept. She texted with it wherever she was, whatever she was doing. She held her breath as she waited for a new message from him, and when she saw it, her heart leapt and her eyes laughed.

The world around Milena was changing before her eyes. Fallen yellow leaves, bare but towering trees, beautiful new buildings, the sights of her favourite city. How could she not have noticed all this beauty before? Had it really been like this in the previous years of her short life? Or has everything changed?

Time had changed its nature. Life had taken on new colours. It had been coloured before, but with the least saturation. And now... . Even on the most cloudy and colourless days, the colours of autumn filled Milena's whole day. The mountain seemed to her like a bold marker that filled her life with the slightest movement.

Milena got up in the morning with her heart beating, expecting more and more miracles and fabulous events from the new day. Things had indeed changed. She realised that. There was a part of her that was afraid, because a new world was opening up before her. But at the same time, she had so much strength and courage that she was ready to move mountains, she was ready to take a step that had seemed impossible before.

She smiled every time she looked in the mirror. Expressive brown eyes, long thick lashes, a small nose, juicy symmetrical lips, pronounced cheekbones, long silky golden hair.

Milena had always known that she was beautiful. But lately she had noticed features on her face that simply amazed her.

"Is it really me, am I really so beautiful? Has this guy, just by looking at me, made me see something I hadn't noticed in twenty-three years?

Who is he? Could he be an angel who will take me to heaven, or a demon who has decided to take me to his underworld? What should I do? How do I find out? Should I give in to my feelings or stop before it's too late?

Each time Milena repeated these words to herself, and each time, without listening to her own thoughts, she sank deeper into the maelstrom of new feelings.

"Thank you, life. Thank you for giving me this opportunity. I don't know what will come of all this, but I hope for the best, I hope for love".

Milena's lessons have not changed either. Both at the university and on stage she simply shone. She attended lessons and rehearsals with great joy and enthusiasm. The teacher was delighted to see such excellent changes in his student. She always had a good voice, even the most difficult songs were easy for her. But the soul she put into her music had not been noticed for a long time. And now in every song, in every note, deep feelings and life were manifested.

Gor: "I think we can get together as a group.

Milena: "I agree, it's a good idea. Let's talk to the boys and decide".

Gor: "What is there to say? We'll decide for ourselves and we'll tell them the time and place right away".

Milena: "We can do it like that.

Gor: "Sure. We'll arrange everything."

Milena: "Good."

Milena herself was not aware of how easily and casually she agreed with him on everything. The conversations were mostly about nothing. He didn't talk much about himself, and Milena was afraid to talk about herself, although he had never asked her about anything in particular. She wanted to know all about him. To get inside his head and hear what he breathed, what he lived.

Milena waited with bated breath to meet him. His face was fading from her memory. That's why she looked at his photos on Facebook every day, so that his image would always be with her.

Astine uploaded photos of Armen's birthday. Milena spent hours looking at them. He, she, together. At least in the photo, but together. It turned out that they were standing next to each other everywhere. Two tall, handsome figures. "How we fit together. How beautiful we look."

Gor: "Nice birthday photos"

Milena: "I agree with you. I like them too"

Gor: "They turned out great. You look very beautiful."

Milena: "Thank you. You too."

Gor: "Thank you. I know."

Milena: ")))))"

Every day. Every hour. He became her obsession, following her everywhere. On the street, when she suddenly saw a similar silhouette, her heart jumped, her breathing quickened. But when she realised she was wrong again, she calmed down and continued on her way.

More than once she imagined her future with him: meeting him, kissing him, meeting his parents, getting engaged, getting married, living together, having children – everything possible. Girls are like that, once they fall in love, the world will change, they will change. They will dream and dream of something that does not exist. Milena was well aware of all this, she knew that she should not be so weak, so easy and simple to give her heart to an almost stranger, to bind herself to him, but she could not help it.

The feelings were stronger.

Gor: "I'm so tired of cold weather before it starts.

Milena: "Yes? I think so."

Gor: "Especially with winter and New Year's Eve coming up. I don't feel like it."

Milena: "Well, yes. Maybe."

But she loved winter so much. She loved New Year's Eve so much. The magic, the snow, the whiteness, the miracles. She loved it all so much.

Chapter 5

2014. Early December

*Music inspires the whole world, supplies the soul with wings,
encourages the flight of imagination; music gives life and cheerfulness
to everything in existence...
It can be called the embodiment of all that is beautiful
and all that is sublime.*
— Plato

– Music is something lifeless. But it has more life and soul than any of us. It can give us life, love, and emotion. It can make the impossible possible. It can change the whole world around us, change our perception of it. It can sharpen all the feelings a human being is capable of. It can give hope or take it away. It can give happiness or take it away after it has reached its peak. From the very first notes, it can bring back memories from distant and forgotten depths or plunge us into the abyss of oblivion and tranquillity. Music is powerful. It can do anything. And only by finding the right note, the right melody, can you reach the highest. To the heights you thought you could never reach.

Every lesson with Karina, a small, full–bodied woman of about forty–five, with the most beautiful features, short black hair pulled back in a bun, began with these words. The students knew her every word by heart, but still they listened with the attention they deserved. She taught them to appreciate the unique energy and power of music. They learned to use the notes for sublime and unearthly purposes. They learned to love and to win. Music gave them more than they could have known and perceived without it.

Vocal lessons, which took up all of Milena's free time, brought happiness and a sense of fulfilment to her life. Every day after finishing her lessons at the medical school, she would drive to the private music school for another lesson and rehearsal. And on weekends, when the doors of the university were closed, Milena opened the doors of the music school with great pleasure, which always waited for her with open arms.

– My dear, you've been singing since you were a nappy. You started singing before you could talk. You just have a unique, magical voice. And you know it. I just don't get it, I don't get it, for the life of me. It's been so many years, and I don't understand why the hell you want to go to med school. Didn't you have anything else to spoil your life with? You're strange, Milena, very strange.

– My dear Karina, I've known you for so many years, and not a day goes by since I started medical school that you don't remind me of my decision. And my answer is always the same: I love medicine, I love music. I can't imagine my life without either one. One complements the other, making it deeper and more interesting.

– Okay, okay. I can't argue with you. You tell me another thing, – suddenly said Karina, sharply looking Milena in the eyes, – what is that shining in your eyes? Did something happen that I don't know about yet?

Karina spoke with such confidence and conviction that whatever Milena was hiding, she would surely tell her everything.

– No, Karina. Not at all, said Milena, a little embarrassed to have revealed her secret.

– But before I had my doubts, and now I'm sure. Spit it out. I'm looking forward to it.

Milena did not hesitate for long. After all, she and Karina had more than just a business relationship. During all their years of study, Milena and Karina had become good and loyal friends, despite the big age difference.

– Oh my God, Milena. I'm so happy, – Karina exclaimed enthusiastically as soon as Milena had finished her story, – I was afraid this day would never come. You're such a beautiful girl in every way that it's people like you who don't find the right partner in life. And spend their whole lives alone with their careers and their families.

– To be honest, Karina, I also thought I would choose the career path, but when I met him, my whole inner world changed. My views, my attitude to people changed. He has filled my whole life, Karina.

– Milena, I'm so happy for you. But, my dear, even though you're no longer a child, he is your first true love. Please don't give yourself completely to him. Keep something for yourself. Men, of course, give us immense happiness, but the pain inflicted by them is incomparable to anything. So, no matter what happens, never love anyone more than yourself. You are still young and may not understand me, but believe me, time will come, you will remember my words. God grant that you will never feel this pain, that next to your chosen one you will always shine with happiness.

– Thank you, Karina. I'll take your words to heart. But I don't think he's like that. He won't hurt me.

– God willing, my dear, God willing.

Milena knew in detail about Karina's private life. How she, after ten years of marriage to the man she loved, had caught him with a work colleague in her flat, in her bed. She left her husband immediately, without thinking for a second. They had no children. It was just the way it was. Karina spent a long time in a rehabilitation centre. According to her, it was music that saved her. It was music that pulled her out of the clutches of death. For although Karina was breathing and her heart was beating, she was dead.

The doctor who treated her played music by the best composers in Karina's room every day. And every day he noticed more and more changes for the better in her. He realised that medication was ineffective in this case. That something intangible and magical would bring her out of this state.

After a few months of rehabilitation, Karina was in better shape. The doctor treating her after she was discharged watched Carina for a long time until one day he made her his wife.

Karen and Karina became a unique pair. They complemented each other as only love films can. A year later their first child was born. Throughout the ten years she spent with her ex–husband, Karina thought she was infertile. But fate had a unique surprise for her.

Karen and Karina have been happily married for fifteen years and have raised three beautiful children.

Chapter 6

2014. Mid–December

Don't look for the light outside – it's within you.
Don't look for happiness in another – it's in your eyes.
Don't look for sweet words – they are on your lips.
Don't look for common sense – it's in your head.
Don't look for love in the unworthy – it's in your heart.
Don't look for support from those around you – it's in your hands.
Don't look for beauty in flowers – it's in your soul.
Don't look for the meaning of life anywhere – you are life.
—— Lusine Aleksanyan

– My beauty. Oh God, how beautiful you are, – Astine hugged her friend tightly.

– Thank you, my Astine.

– Hello, Milena. You look beautiful.

– Hello, Armen. Thank you very much.

Milena and Armen also hugged each other.

– The dress is amazing, Milena, – Astine couldn't stop admiring her friend.

The long, airy dress made of yellow shimmering chiffon, leather shoes of the same colour with high heels, earrings and a ring with yellow and gold sparkling stones made Milena's picture really unique.

Milena looked around with a curiosity that was not lost on Astine. She looked at her friend questioningly. It was only when she met her gaze that she realised what her friend's concern meant.

– He's not here, – Astine said, moving her lips so that Armen wouldn't hear.

Milena knew perfectly well that he wasn't here, that he hadn't come. But she was so reluctant to accept the reality. She had hoped that he would appear at the door at any moment. But... .

The drip of sadness was replaced by a fountain of despair. Milena's heart clenched. Her throat went dry. She realised she couldn't sing like that.

"Milena, pull yourself together. Today is an important day. Please pull yourself together. You have to perform beautifully. Oh, God. My ring finger is numb again. "Why am I so nauseous? What's wrong with me?"

– Milena, are you all right? Shall I get you some water? Armen, darling, get some water quickly.

Astine held Milena's wrist as if to keep her from falling. Armen wanted to get some water, but Milena stopped him.

– Armen, wait. Don't go. It's all right now. I'm fine. I was just dizzy. I'm fine now.

– Milena, are you sure? – asked Armen as he came over to Milena.

– Milena, darling, can we cancel the show?

– No, guys. Thank you very much. But it's okay. Really.

Milena straightened up and started to fix her hair and dress when she suddenly heard the voice of one of the workers backstage:

– Milena, you're on in five minutes.

– Okay, – Milena said and took a deep breath.

– That's it, Milena, we're going to take our seats. Your parents and Ani are already in the hall. Are you sure you're alright?

– Yes, of course, go ahead. Yes, Astine, take it easy. Thank you for everything.

The friends hugged each other again.

– Good luck, my dear.

– Good luck, Milena.

– Thanks, guys.

Milena led the lovers to the door and headed for the stage. It was time for her to go. She took small steps along the stage and stopped in the middle. The auditorium was dark. She couldn't see anyone. The music poured out in a stream. Irina Allegrova's "Flood". She gripped the microphone with both hands, raised it to her lips, closed her eyes, took a deep breath and surrendered to the song.

Exhale. Fingers slightly relaxed. Eyes open.

Rumble applause. The audience is on its feet. "Bravo! Well done! Hooray!"

Goosebumps run down Milena's body. Excited, she looked at the audience. The lights came on in time. She saw her parents: her mother with eyes full of tears, her proud but no less excited father. Ani, Astine, Armen applauded their friend with smiles. Milena watched. Her breath caught. Her heart pounded. Her lips smiled involuntarily. Her soul immediately became warm and pleasant.

– You've come, – her smiling lips whispered softly. – You're here.

It seemed to her that he applauded louder than anyone else, that he smiled wider than anyone else, that his eyes were full of light and radiance that reflected all around. She couldn't take her eyes off him, couldn't stop her heart from racing. She was full of happiness, admiration and love. She was in love. She was in love.

After the concert, when Milena took off her costume and put on jeans, a blue jumper, red suede boots and a blue and red duffle jacket, she found her friends and parents waiting for her at the entrance to the concert hall. He was standing on the edge, next to Armen, still smiling at her. She couldn't believe her eyes, couldn't believe that he was there, right next to her. Standing with her parents. "I wonder if they've had a chance to meet?" A question that never left Milena's mind for a moment.

Hugs, congratulations, real praise. A huge bouquet of her favourite white roses from her parents and red roses from her friends. He stood there empty–handed, just smiling. But that was enough for her. His mere presence was enough to make her completely happy. "He's here. He's near."

Some time passed after the concert. Milena saw Gor a few more times. But as usual, they were in the company of mutual friends. He was very polite to her, friendly, but nothing more. The virtual communication continued as before, but there was nothing concrete to suggest something more, a further relationship. And what Milena had waited for so long, with all her heart and being, did not happen. But she had dreamed so much of it.

Chapter 7

2015. January

*If a man has one thought,
he finds it in everything.*
— B. Hugo.

The day was coming to an end and Milena could not get the events of the morning out of her mind. Her heart could not rest.

The usual text message:

"Hi, Milena. How are you? Happy New Year. I wish you all the best this year".

Typical reply:

"Hi, Gor. Thank you very much. I am very touched. Happy New Year to you too. May all your hopes and dreams come true."

Two lines of correspondence and she's in seventh heaven. Two lines of correspondence and it's the best New Year's Eve she's had in the last twenty–three years.

The next morning Milena was awakened by a knock at the door. She jumped from her seat in surprise. "Who could it be so early in the morning?" But before Milena could get out of bed, she heard her father's heavy footsteps outside her room, followed a second later by the sound of the front door lock opening.

Milena tried to strain her hearing, but apart from "...yes, you came right away... I'm her father... she's still sleeping... okay...

and from whom? ...okay... goodbye" and the sound of the door closing, Milena heard nothing else. She was still trying to guess who was coming and why, when suddenly her father appeared on the threshold of her room.

– Good morning, darling, – he said as he entered the room.

– Hello, Daddy. What's that in your hand?

Milena was sitting in bed, wrapped in a warm blanket.

– I don't know. Maybe you can tell me.

Her father handed Milena a small grey box without a lid, inside of which was a grey Me to You bear, surrounded by countless Kinder chocolates, every girl's favourite treat.

– As you guessed, this is for you, – her father said.

Milena took the box from her father, but instead of being happy about the gift, she tried to find something.

– The gift is anonymous," said the father, anticipating his daughter's gesture. "I looked. There's no note. And the delivery man didn't want to share the information.

– Strange, – said Milena, putting on a mask of indifference. But in her soul, she was happy, her heart was beating.

"It's him, it's him. Is it really him?" Milena was filled with positive emotions just thinking about it, rejoiced with all her heart, but tried her best not to show her feelings, lest her father suddenly suspect something.

– Well, young lady? What are your thoughts and suspicions about your secret admirer?

– None, Papa. Not the slightest doubt who it could be, – Milena replied with a peculiar indifference.

– I see. Well, I'll be going. I'll leave you to your chocolates. But, I warn you, – he said in a serious voice, – leave some for me and Mum, we like them too.

Seeing the serious look on his daughter's face, her father smiled and she smiled back. He left the room, closing the door behind him. He gave no sign that he didn't believe his daughter's words. Her eyes were shining as only eyes full of love and happiness can shine.

The New Year holidays are over. Classes start again. A cycle of psychiatry in one of the city's psychiatric hospitals. The teacher is a young, but intelligent, smiling man of short stature with golden hair combed back.

– Yes, boys, I've checked everyone's tests. Here are your answers, – he said, handing out the sheets.

The psychological test carried out during the lesson was as follows: the teacher showed pictures with unintelligible images and each student described what he saw in the picture on his sheet of paper. Then the teacher, after reading the product of the students' imagination, deduced the psychological conclusion of each student.

And so, all the students received their answer sheets except one. Milena kept waiting for the teacher to get her sheet. But he remained silent. Her friends, not paying attention, read their answers with great enthusiasm.

Milena did not dare to ask the teacher where her test was, she just looked at him questioningly. When he saw her look, he knew what she was hiding.

– Milena, I will give you the answer to your test orally. If it's convenient for you, stay after class, – he said in a calm, quiet voice.

Surprised, Milena did not dare to answer. She just nodded in agreement.

After the lesson, Milena warned her friends that she would be a little longer and asked them not to wait for her. They were reluctant to leave their friend alone in the hospital.

– You're probably wondering, – he began in the same calm, quiet voice when he and Milena were alone in the classroom, "why I did that."

– Honestly, yes, – Milena replied shyly.

– I won't try your patience, – he continued without changing his tone. – To be honest, I wasn't surprised when I read your notes. Strangely enough, I saw in you at first glance what made you different from the others. Yes, Milena, don't be surprised, but you really are different from many of your peers. You are one of the few, very few, especially nowadays, who are spiritual people.

– I don't understand you, – Milena said in surprise.

– It's all right, I'll explain.

She nodded. He continued.

– You are a very sensitive and vulnerable person. But that doesn't mean you're not strong. There are so many paradoxes about you. You're like a sponge. You absorb every emotion, every action, every feeling. That's why you sing. I've heard you sing. It has nothing to do with good singing skills. Lots of people sing. But what you experience with every song, not everyone can do. I noticed that right away.

Milena listened quietly and attentively to the young teacher, not wanting to interrupt him.

– Milena, there aren't many like you. Whatever happens, don't lose yourself. Stay as you are now. Life will hurt your fragile soul more than once. But I'm sure that even this will not be your downfall, but your elevation.

Milena left the hospital confused. She didn't understand how her answers to this routine test had managed to characterise her in such detail. For a long time, Milena replayed the teacher's words in her mind, each time more surprised than the last.

It was St Sargis Day, the feast of lovers in Armenia. On the night of the holiday, unmarried and single young people eat something called a "salted pancake" and then go to bed without drinking water. It is believed that whoever gives water in a dream is sent by fate.

Milena and her brother ate a salted pancake prepared by their mother every year. Aren saw a different girl every year, which made his parents jokingly angry. Milena had the opposite idea. She never saw anyone. In her dreams, she poured water for herself and drank the long-awaited liquid. But still Milena ate the fateful pancake every year.

A dark, dense forest. She stands by the path, unable to move. But it's not fear that keeps her still. A stream flows beside her. She is thirsty. But her body does not listen, does not obey her will. She just stands there, staring at the spring with greedy eyes. Suddenly, two boys stand in front of her. She can't see their faces in the darkness. She squints her eyes, but to no avail. The silhouettes look familiar, but she can't remember them. One of the boys, coming to the spring, fills a wooden glass to the brim and holds it out to her. But she doesn't even notice what he's doing. She can't take her eyes off the other man, who is still standing, unmoving, with the glass in his hand. She slowly approaches him, takes his free hand and leads him to the spring. He fills the water halfway and holds the glass out to her. She takes the glass and takes her time. She fills the glass to the brim and then greedily drinks the water down to the last drop. And the man with the wooden glass continues to stand there with his hand outstretched.

– Hello, darling, – said Astine as she came into Milena's house.

– Hello, my darling. Come in, – said Milena and closed the front door.

Astine took off her coat and scarf and walked through the large entrance hall into the spacious living room. A tea table with all sorts of goodies was set up in front of the friends' favourite sofa.

– Sit down, Astine, I'll pour the tea and come over.

A minute later Milena came into the living room with two large mugs in her hands.

– Well, – she said, putting the glasses down and sitting down next to her friend.

– Oh, I forgot. Happy holidays.

– Happy holidays, Astine. I can't forget what day it is. Ever since last night, this day has been reminding me of itself.

– What do you mean? What happened?

Without answering, Milena looked at the huge bouquet of white roses on the large table. Astine looked at Milena with big eyes.

– Is this for you? From whom?

– I don't know. It arrived this morning. Again, no addressee. I don't know, Astine. Is it him? I hope it's him. It's just that we haven't spoken in a few days. So, I'm afraid to guess.

– It's strange, Milena. I don't know what to say. You know, the thing that surprises me most is that Armen doesn't know anything. That's what worries me the most. I hinted at the first gift, but he was completely in the dark. That's why I didn't continue.

Milena looked at the bouquet in silence.

– It's beautiful.

– Yes, – agreed Milena. – My favourite white roses.

The friends sat in silence for a few minutes, drinking tea and admiring the flowers.

– Oh, Astine, I completely forgot. I haven't told you about my dream.

– Come on. In detail, – said Astine, making herself comfortable.

Milena told her friend about her strange dream.

– I've never had dreams like that before, Astine. I don't know what to think.

– Yes, it's strange. What surprised me the most were the glasses. Glass and wood. What could that mean? Oh, Milena, you're always so strange, – Astine said with a laugh.

– You don't say. Where are you and Armen going today?

– I don't know. He said it was a surprise. He's going to pick me up at seven and take me somewhere I don't know.

– That's great. I'm so happy for you, Astine. You're so happy around him. You always light up when you're with him. That's the most important thing.

– Yes, Milena, I'm happy. And I want you to be happy too.

– Me too, Astine, me too, – Milena said, looking at the bouquet. Her eyes sparkled, her lips smiled.

"I'm already happy."

Chapter 8

2015. February

Love like a shadow flies when substance love pursues;
Pursuing that that flies, and flying what pursues.
—William Shakespeare

– I don't know what to think, girls. He sent me two presents and acts as if nothing has happened.

The friends were sitting in a small, warm, cosy café on Northern Avenue. At a small table by the window. It was dry but cold outside. There was no snow in sight.

– We were still socialising as before. But I thought after he sent the gift and then the bouquet, he would do something. But he didn't. And I don't dare say anything myself.

– Milena, of course I don't want to say anything. I just don't have a choice.

Astine and Milena looked carefully at Ani, who spoke to their great surprise. Ani continued, slightly embarrassed.

– Milena, I'm sorry in advance.

– Well, Ani, you are slow. Come on, – Astine couldn't bear it.

– What if it's not him? – Ani said.

Milena lowered her head.

– To be honest, girls, I've thought about it too. But I didn't dare admit it, not even to myself.

– Milena, do you have any other ideas who it could be?

Astine had thought about it too, but she didn't want to disappoint her friend. So, she kept quiet.

– No, Astine. I have no idea who it could be. Neither gift was a random choice. The person who gave them knew what I loved. And I've only talked about it with Horus. Otherwise.

– Yes. I don't know what to think, – I said to Astine.

– I don't know either, – Ani agreed.

As the girls finished their tea in silence, Ani checked the latest gossip on Facebook.

– Oh, have you heard the latest news? – she asked suddenly.

– What news? – Milena was interested.

– Do you remember our classmate Maria?

– The tall one?

– Yes.

– Well, yes. She was born on the same day as me, – said Milena, remembering their meeting in the lift. – What happened to her?

– Her boyfriend proposed to her in Tsakhkadzor. She accepted. They put the video on the internet, but the connection is so bad that it won't load.

– No matter, we'll watch it at home, – said Astine indifferently.

– I'm happy for her. She's pretty. She's very pretty. Let her be happy, – Milena's voice trembled. But her words were sincere.

– Mm–hmm, – Ani agreed, 'not taking her eyes off the screen of her phone.

Milena imagined this picture. How romantic it all was. She had always dreamed of going to Tsakhkadzor in winter, where there was no shortage of snow. And where there was snow, there were wonders. But her trip was never to happen.

– The white–skinned beauty got what I dream of every day. At least let her enjoy this unique happiness.

Milena's eyes wept, goose bumps ran down her body. She smiled as she swallowed her last sip of tea.

She walked into the classroom, as always, with a smile on her face. And he, as always, was waiting for her with a swoon in his heart and happiness in his eyes. The scent of her perfume filled the room as soon as she crossed the threshold. He admired every part of her: what she was wearing, the jewellery she had chosen to match her outfit, her shoes and her bag. He admired her always beautifully styled golden hair, her delicate make–up, her always manicured nails.

He noticed the smallest detail in her, but she only saw his silhouette. He loved and she only smiled. He admired her and she was silent.

Love makes you see the invisible, broadens your horizons, changes and enriches your view of the world.

– Hi, Milena, – said Tigran, smiling as soon as Milena crossed the threshold of the classroom.

– Hi, Tigran, – she replied, looking at him only briefly.

– How are you doing?

– Fine, thank you. And you?

– Me too.

He couldn't take his eyes off her. He savoured her every move. As she took off her coat, her scarf, as she put on her medical gown, sat down in her seat, took a pen and a small notebook from her pocket, tucked her hair behind her ear, he recorded it all, filed it away in the recesses of his memory.

The fair–skinned, good–looking, blue–eyed boy of small stature, with a handsome, athletic build, had studied with her in the same group for almost two years. He had liked her at first sight. But he hadn't paid any attention. And he hadn't paid any attention to her until recently, when he realised that the short New Year holidays were a long time for him to be away from her, that he needed her like a breath of fresh air. He knew everything about her. Her tastes, her interests. She'd discussed them with her friends more than once, and he'd been drawn to her every word like a magnet.

Unable to resist any longer, he decided to make the first move and send her a small New Year's Eve present, knowing in advance how much she would like it. He wanted to leave a note to let her know from whom the surprise was, but at the last moment he changed his mind and took out a small envelope. And he forbade the courier to mention his name under any pretext.

He knew she had received the gift and he knew she had no idea it was from him. And yet he continued to love her in silence. After a while he sent her a bouquet of her favourite white roses. Again, only silence accompanied the queens of flowers.

They were alone in the hall. He had come early on purpose, knowing in advance that she would not be late. And knowing the character of his classmates, who were always punctual, he looked at his watch and realised that he had about ten minutes. Ten minutes to say all the things he had been silent about for so long.

– Milena, if you're not too busy, can we talk? – he said, taking a deep breath.

Milena put her phone down and looked at Tigran carefully.

– Yes, of course, I'm listening.

– I don't even know where to begin. I've been languishing for so long.

– Start at the beginning, – Milena said confidently, smiling slightly.

Tigran was embarrassed. He tried hard to collect himself and speak.

– I like you, Milena, – he said sharply.

Milena looked at him astonished. She had never thought of such a thing. She was at a loss for words. He used her silence to continue.

– I've always had feelings for you. I've been silent for too long. I've never been able to talk to you, to open up to you. But now I think the time has come. I'm very fond of you, Milena. You're the beautiful girl I want to spend the rest of my life with. You're unique. Enchanting.

– That's enough, Tigran. Don't.

Milena got up, went to the window and stood with her back to Tigran.

– Milena, please don't be so harsh. Listen to me.

– Tigran, – she began, turning to face him, – forgive me for being sharp and direct, but I can't help it. I don't want you to continue this conversation. For your own good.

– Milena, I really like you, – he tried to speak calmly, but the tremor in his voice wouldn't go away. – Give me a chance. I'm not asking for much. Just a date to get to know each other. Not as classmates, just as boyfriend and girlfriend, outside of these hospitals and clinics.

– Are you ready? – She said suddenly. He nodded. She continued, – Now listen to me, Tigran. I'm only going to say this once. I don't like to repeat myself. I don't like you. Not at all. You're a nice guy, but you're not for me. There's no point in starting anything, because nothing on my part will change. And your feelings will only get worse. I don't want to play with your feelings and get your hopes up. So, don't say another word about it. Do you understand me?

– How can you be so sure? You don't know me at all, do you?

– Maybe, but I know me.

– I need a chance, Milena. Just one date.

– Not one, Tigran. This is my last word. Don't ever bring this up again. Nothing will change, ever.

Tigran was stunned. He had not expected such words and such an answer from a fragile, delicate girl. He was depressed. But he tried not to show it.

– And the presents? Didn't you like them?

Milena smiled slightly. Ani was right.

– Very much, but if I had known they were from you, I would have sent them back.

– Oh my God, Milena. What's wrong with you? I don't recognise you. – Tigran raised his voice in anger and despair.

– Don't shout. We're in a hospital. Maybe you never knew me, Tigran. White roses don't mean you know me. You've got to understand that.

– Am I that bad, Milena? – he said with a special calm and a painful look in his eyes that Milena could not escape.

– No, Tigran, – she began calmly. – If I don't reciprocate, that doesn't mean you're bad. No. You're really a very nice guy. But you're not right for me. I don't have to go out with you to see that. I can tell just by looking at you. I'm sure you'll find the right girl to give you true love and happiness.

– But, Milena.

– Hi guys.

Astine suddenly entered the auditorium, went over to her friend and kissed her.

– Hi, Astine.

– Is something wrong? – asked Astine, who couldn't escape her friend's gaze.

– Yes, no. Nothing is wrong.

The audience began to fill. Soon the teacher entered and began the lesson. Milena glanced at Tigran from time to time, knowing full well that he avoided her gaze. She could sense that he wasn't feeling well, but she knew that she had done the right thing. "You'll thank me again, Tigran, that I didn't take advantage of your feelings and hurt you. It's the right thing to do."

She was only proud of those she did not care about. She knew how to say "no" to those for whom her heart was not set. And the slightest emotion made her helpless, docile and unwilling, erasing even the trace of pride that had broken more than one heart.

Chapter 9

2015. February

If you've started tripping over life's minor obstacles;
If you think there is no way out;
if it seems to you that nobody understands you,
doesn't listen and doesn't hear you;
if you want to stop at the very beginning.
turn on a song, the one that you associate with the best
of your life that you've already forgotten.
Already from the first notes everything around you will change.
The sun will shine.
— Lusine Aleksanyan

Rain. One of the few moments when you can stay at home and plunge into a maelstrom of thoughts, dream, listen to your favourite music, drink hot tea and wrap yourself in a warm soft plaid.

Rain. One of the few moments when your best friend is yourself. When you don't want anyone's company, not even your nearest and dearest.

It's raining. Droplets of clear liquid hitting the windows. At such a moment, especially to the rhythm of your favourite music, it seems to you that these little pranksters want to get to the innermost things, the things that are hidden very deep in your heart.

But the song ends, the raindrops fade, unable to beat any further, and you return to the ground, to your room, where you wrap yourself in the same warm blanket and drink your tea, which has already cooled.

And then you realise that it was just rain to the rhythm of your favourite music.

It's ringing. It's an unknown number.

Hello?

Hello.

Tachycardia.

Tachycardia.

How are you?

Lump in my throat.

I'm fine. And you?

Me too. What are you doing?

Chills all over my body.

Oh, I'm just sitting at home. And you?

Sweaty palms.

Me too.

Silence.

All right. I'll call you later. Bye.

Okay. Bye.

Milena put the phone down. An incomprehensible cloudiness enveloped her. "What does it mean? What did he want? I don't understand. It was the first time he called me. But what did his call mean? Jesus, what's going on? What's going on?"

I want so much to walk with him in the centre of the city, holding hands, feeling the warmth of his beloved body, inhaling the smell of his cologne and the rain–wet asphalt. I'd like that so much.

A few days later, Milena received an invitation from Astine to spend a Saturday night in one of the capital's Spanish clubs. Milena was reluctant but accepted her friend's offer, not wanting to miss out on her favourite Latin American dances.

As Milena entered the club, the group of friends was already assembled. She glanced around the group with bated breath, looking for him. But her expectations were not fulfilled. Her sad eyes faded. Although the Spanish rhythms left no one indifferent, Milena could not get herself to dance. Her friends were on the dance floor, and Milena finished another glass of beer, admiring the couples dancing passionately.

– Hi.

Milena put down her glass, hesitating to turn her head. But there was no need to, for the owner of the voice was standing next to her. She was speechless when she saw him and swallowed her saliva with difficulty.

– I didn't think you would come.

– I didn't think I would either. I had things to do. I got off early.

Milena looked at the clock. 22:25. Wow, early.

– Why aren't you dancing? No date? – he said with a grin.

– No, I'm not. I just don't feel like it, – Milena replied, taking a sip of beer.

Gor, not answering, called the waiter over and placed his order.

A minute later the waiter returned with two glasses of beer.

– Here's to you, – Gor said, raising his glass. He drained it in seconds.

Milena watched every sip, every tiny movement.

– Shall we dance?

She didn't have time to answer, but Gor took her hand and pulled her to the dance floor. Milena stood alone for a moment while Gor greeted the boys. After greeting everyone, he returned to her, took her hands in his and pressed her light, feathery body passionately against his.

Prince Royce – Darte un Beso. Bachata. A dance that brings together not only bodies but also souls. A dance that doesn't leave anyone indifferent. A dance that makes you not only feel, but love.

During the dance, she kept trying to talk to him. To talk about this strange phone call. But she couldn't find the words. Next to him, she was speechless and just plain stupid.

Midnight.

– I'll see you out.

– Are you sure? Wouldn't it be better if I took a taxi?

– Do I seem insecure?

– No, it's not that. It's just that...

– If it's not that, then get in the car.

His confident voice didn't allow Milena to argue or disobey. She loved his determination, his unflinching gaze. He would possess her before he could even touch her. And she would give herself to him only when she met the gaze of his black eyes.

After saying goodbye to the boys, they got into Gor's black Mercedes.

She fastened her seatbelt. He – unbuckled, looking at her intently. She didn't even argue. And yet she had always obeyed the law. She'd always done the right thing.

He turned on the music. How strange. Her favourite song. ARTIK & ASTI– Winter. He drove slowly. The music, the dark night, his presence, his smell, his breath, his heartbeat involved Milena in something indescribable. Painfully pleasurable.

She felt the warmth of his hand as he took her left hand in his with particular tenderness. She looked at him. He looked back. He drove with one hand, still holding her hand.

She looked ahead, at the road. But her mind was with him. The song "Winter" was replaced by "So It Was" by the same duo. He lifted her hand and brought it to his lips. A shiver ran through Milena's body as she felt the warmth of his lips on her hand. That look again. Eyes glistening. Bodies on fire.

They turned off the road and drove another hundred metres before the car stopped. Milena's breathing quickened.

– Why did you stop? – she asked, not looking in his direction.

He was silent. She only felt his breath close to her. His lips were on her left ear. She closed her eyes. Her lips parted slightly.

– It's late. I have to go home, – she whispered.

He was silent. His lips moved slowly down her neck. They moved up to her cheek, moving gently to her eager lips.

"Would this really be the first time, here, now, with him? Would he really be the one to give my lips their first long–awaited kiss?"

Milena's thoughts were interrupted by Gor's hand running lightly through her hair, then down her cheek, taking her chin and turning her head affectionately to the left. She met his black eyes. They were filled with passion, with desire.

His lips touched hers gently, capturing her lips with a special passion. She felt the warmth of his lips, his hands caressing her body. Her hands sank into his close–cropped hair. The passion grew with every movement. His scent drove her mad. The song replaced one another. Everything around her changed. She changed.

When the car stopped near her house, he gave her another unforgettable kiss. She smiled slightly. He smiled back.

"Good night," he said. Two words for the whole unforgettable hour they spent alone together. Two words for all the times of happiness.

"Good night," she said. And closing the car door behind her, she flew home.

The days passed. Milena woke up each day with anticipation. She waited for at least some movement from him. But all she got was silence. She couldn't forgive herself for that night. She didn't even want to think that he had just played a cruel joke on her, that everything that had happened had been the result of the effects of alcohol. She was devastated, crushed. She checked his page every day, looking for any hint of what had happened. But the page was blank. The green circle next to his name said he was in a chat room. But there were still no letters from him. She was afraid, hesitant to speak, hesitant to write to him herself, hesitant to overcome her ego. But her heart clenched in her chest, she was always short of breath, her thoughts never left her. And all the time he remained silent.

Chapter 10

2015. The beginning of March

> *...And when the heart bursts,*
> *Without a healer to undo the wounds,*
> *— Know that out of the heart there is a head,*
> *And there is an axe – from the head ...*
> *— Marina Tsvetaeva*

– Ast, I swear I don't understand him. There can't be so many contradictions in one man! He changes every minute. I really don't understand what his changes have to do with. Is it his nature, or is it just me?

The friends sat on the comfortable sofa in Milena's living room, listening to music and drinking hot tea. Astine listened attentively, never taking her eyes off her glass. Milena continued.

– Ast, you are the only one who knows in detail what has happened between me and Gor since the day we met. Tell me, where is my mistake? Where exactly did I fail? Was I wrong to respond to his kiss? But damn it, Astine, it was the best day of my life. I don't regret it and I never will.

Milena leaned back on the back of the couch, hugging a small decorative pillow.

– No, Milena. You didn't make a mistake. You did what your heart told you to do, and that's what any young girl would do. It's something else entirely.

– What is it, Ast? What's wrong with me? What's wrong with him?

Astine was silent for a moment, as if thinking.

– Milena, I've wanted to tell you something about Gor for a long time, but I've been hesitant to tell you. When you two started talking, I thought he'd tell you sooner or later. But I don't know if I should.

– Astine, if you know something important that I need to know, please tell me. It's very important to me.

– Yes, Milena, I understand, I just don't know if I have the right to discuss someone else's private life, even with a close friend.

– Astine, you won't do anything wrong. I won't even pretend to know anything. Please tell me. My heart is about to jump out of my chest.

– I don't know.

Milena rose from her seat, crouched down in front of Astine, took her hands in hers and looked into her friend's pleading eyes. There was so much emotion in those soft, beautiful brown eyes that Astine gave in, unable to bear her friend's gaze for even a minute.

–Stand up, Milena. Sit next to me. All right, – Astine began, taking a deep breath, – I'll tell you everything. Just promise me that after you've heard everything, you won't jump to any conclusions, let alone take any action.

–I promise, – Milena said and sat down in her old place.

–Then I'll start, – Astine said, pausing for a moment, – I learned everything, of course, from Armen. He told me Gor's story quite by accident. That day we were at Gor's birthday party, they were both drunk, they had a little argument over nothing. Afterwards, I decided to take Armen away to avoid making things worse. We decided to go for a walk before going home, and Armen poured out his feelings to me, telling me the truth about Gor. The truth that made him what you know him to be.

After entering medical school, Gor set himself another goal – to win the hearts of thousands of medical students. From the first day of school, Gor was the centre of attention not only of his classmates, but also of many older female students. His tall stature, athletic build, black hair and eyes made him an irreplaceable stealer of young hearts. Gor loved the attention of the opposite sex. He never missed a look, a gesture or a smile directed at him. He was convinced that he would never fall in love himself and would only enjoy the one–sided love of young people.

The days passed, day after day. Gor's popularity grew. He was only a freshman, but almost the whole university knew about him. He was like the heroes of Disney cartoons: handsome, popular, strong, attractive.

One day during physical education, when the medical and dental students had to take a combined class due to some schedule changes, Gor saw the one he least wanted to see. The one whose meeting had been fateful for him.

He saw this girl for the first time and was surprised that he hadn't noticed such beauty before. She was from the medical faculty, but he could not believe that he had managed to lose sight of her in six months.

The girl – Nina, that was her name – was really good–looking. She was small in stature, but with a fine figure. Red long wavy hair, big green eyes, a small nose, juicy lips, big firm breasts. Most importantly, she was aware of her beauty, and her unique smile never stopped shining.

Something chirped in Gor's heart at the sight of beauty. It was an unfamiliar and strange feeling. But, at first, he didn't pay the slightest attention to the otherworldly symptoms, to what was about to change his whole life. On that fateful day, he had only one goal – to win the attention of the red–haired girl and make her his next admirer.

But Gor's hopes were not to be fulfilled. The girl paid no attention to him. Throughout the hour spent in the gym, no matter how Gor tried to get her attention, he failed. She just didn't notice him.

Angry, agitated, Gor could not find a place to sit. He was outraged. He could not understand why he had earned the contempt of the future doctor.

From that day on, Gor had a new goal – to do whatever it took to win the girl's unyielding heart. He started by asking her classmates for her first and last name. He found her on Facebook. Once he knew her schedule, he followed her every move. The friends who always accompanied Nina noticed the handsome man more than once. But Nina continued to neglect him. Gor's resentment grew with each meeting, with each ignoring of the girl. Gor didn't even notice how the stranger had become his obsession within a few days. Days and nights were filled with nothing but her red hair and green eyes.

But luckily for Gor, and much to his surprise, she accepted his request to be added as a friend on Facebook. Hope flickered in his soul. But Gor's incessant messages went unanswered. One day he went back to his page and saw a message from Nina Mkhitaryan. His heart began to pound relentlessly, his breathing quickened, his hands trembled. As he clicked on the message to view it, he had only a few seconds to experience feelings he had never experienced before. It was then that he realised he was hopelessly and irrevocably in love.

"Hello." That was the long–awaited message from the beauty.

One word – a thousand emotions, a thousand meanings, a thousand feelings.

In a matter of days, the usual "hello" was followed by all the usual words that were meaningful and indispensable to Gor. After a short period of virtual communication, the long–awaited time of face–to–face meetings arrived.

Next to her, Gor became a completely different person, all others faded away for him. He didn't notice anyone at all. Even the company of his faithful friends was easily exchanged for a meeting with his beloved. Days, weeks, months passed. In love, Gor had long since been replaced by true love, and he never stopped telling Nina about his feelings. Nina treated Gor with the same warmth, although she never said the magic three words. But it was all so beautiful.

The girls who had once been Horus's victims watched the beautiful young couple with envy in their eyes. Their relationship had received enormous publicity throughout the medical community.

Then came the moment of meeting the parents, which passed without incident, much to the girls' delight. At the beginning of the third year, Gor and Nina became engaged.

It was clear to everyone that no earthly or heavenly forces would be able to separate them. But the unexpected happened. In December of that year, Gor received a summons from the military recruitment centre. Ten days later, despite the best efforts of family and friends, Gor was drafted into the army. Parting from Nina was difficult. After almost two years together, they had never parted, and now they were to spend the next two years far away from each other.

As he left, Gor took Nina's hands in his, looked intently into her green eyes and said only two words: "Wait for me." "I will," she replied.

Gor left with a strong hope in his heart that at home, away from his parents, he was waiting for the one who was everything to him. Days passed, day after day. A thousand letters, postcards. It seemed that even distance could not separate them, let alone keep them apart.

A month remained before Gor's arrival. But for unknown reasons he was sent home a whole month early, which was a great rarity. Arriving in the capital without even stopping at his parents' house, Gor went to meet his bride with a trembling heart. A strong embrace, a long kiss – everything was the same as before. It seemed as if nothing had changed. It seemed that it was all over, that the separation would never happen again. Never again.

Sitting in the empty garden, surrounded by bare trees, Gor could not get enough of his beloved. He had expected a thousand words from her, but had received only a few sentences. He waited for a passionate, longing look, and received only a green void. Gor sensed something had changed. She had changed. But he didn't want to believe it. Just thinking about it made him sick to his stomach.

But he couldn't avoid what had to happen. After a strained silence, Nina took the ring off her ring finger and placed it in Gor's manly palm. She didn't explain, just mumbled: "I'm sorry. We're too different. I don't want to drag this out for nothing. We have no future together." The stunned Gor continued to sit with his hand outstretched, the rounded metal cooling in it.

Without a word, Nina got into the first taxi and drove off. Coming to his senses, Gor tried to find her. Her phone was silent, she was not at home, her parents were worried, and her Facebook page had been deleted.

After a few days of searching, Gor discovered that Nina had run away with a rich drug addict. The girl's parents were devastated. They repeatedly tried to meet Gor to ask him to apologise for their daughter's shameless act. But Gor never wanted to meet them.

After the news broke, Gor disappeared for a week. Neither his family nor his friends knew where he was. He was found by police officers in a club in the city. Gor had spent a whole week going from one club to another. He was unconscious when they found him. He was taken to hospital, where he spent a long time regaining his strength under the careful care of doctors. But even after his body had fully recovered and he returned home, he was in a state of stupor. He wouldn't talk to anyone, eat or drink. Until his strength left him again and he was back in hospital.

It took a long time for Gor to recover, thanks to the hard work of his parents and friends. Gradually, his senses returned. But the faded sparkle in his eyes could not be restored.

After a few years, Gor returned to his normal life. There was still no shortage of girls. He began to use each of them with renewed vigour, squeezing their strength, their beauty, their love. Those who were lucky enough to fall in love with him were left heartbroken at best.

His disrespectful attitude towards the opposite sex more than once became the subject of great arguments and fights. But he never changed. Friends were afraid for him, afraid even to give him advice, afraid that he had not slipped back into a depressive state.

And the young, handsome man's heart was still bleeding from the unhealed wound.

When Astine had finished her story, she looked at her friend. Her eyes were red with tears. Her whole body trembled. Scared, Astine rushed to her friend and embraced her.

– I'm sorry, Milena, I'm sorry. I didn't mean to tell you all this. I didn't want to hurt you. Please, I'm sorry.

Milena hugged her friend and cried her eyes out.

– I love him, Astine. I love him with all my being. I love him because I know what he's like. Now I know it's not his fault that he's like this. It's not his fault.

– Milena, darling, cry, calm down. Now that you know the truth, you must forget him. He's incapable of love, my love. That word, that feeling, no longer exists for him. He's nothing but a selfish, heartless man. He's not worthy of you.

– No, no... don't say that... no...

– It's all my fault, if I'd told you sooner none of this would have happened. You wouldn't be in so much pain now. I'm sorry, darling, I'm sorry.

Not a day went by that Milena didn't think of Gor and the green–eyed girl. There were conflicting feelings inside Milena that she didn't talk to anyone about. There was an accumulation of love that was burning her from within. She weighed the pros and cons and hesitated to act. She felt that she was not just another suitor for Gor. She felt that there was something between them. She knew it. She was preparing to take the most responsible and important step of her life. She was languishing. She was making up her mind. She decided.

Chapter 11

2015. The middle of March

Love hurts even the gods.
— Petronius

"Hello. How are you? Haven't spoken in a long time. I don't know where to start. I guess I'll start at the beginning. You know, to be honest, there's something I've been wanting to talk to you about for a while, but I've been hesitant to. I know I'll regret it, and I still do, but deep down I feel like I have to. Because otherwise, if I keep silent again, I'll regret it a lot more.

I remember the first day we met. I don't know about you, but I remember it in every detail. I don't think you were as affected by that day as I was. Do you? Am I right? That was the day I realised I was hopelessly and irrevocably in love. Forgive me for my frankness and my sentimentality. But I can't keep quiet any longer.

Not much time had passed, only four months, which seemed like an eternity. In that eternity, I've changed a lot. You changed me without ever playing a role in my life. Maybe without even knowing it. I'm not blaming you or forcing you to do anything. I don't know what's going on. I don't know how I can write this. But my fingers don't obey me. My heart moves them.

I have another confession to make. I know about your lost love. Again, I'm sorry. I don't want to hurt you. I know what it is to love pain. It's the best and the worst feeling in the world. I didn't understand you before. I couldn't understand your behaviour. You paradoxically made me feel happy and desperate. I thought it was me, that I didn't deserve your love. But when I learned the truth, I somehow calmed down. I know now that I'm not the problem. It's just that the disappointment has got the best of you. It's overcome you. You know that yourself. I'm not going to judge you. It's not for me to do that.

But having loved you for such a short time, I saw in you a light that shone through the veil of disappointment. It gave me hope that all was not lost. That you could still love and that I would be the second love of your life.

God, I can't believe I'm writing this. I just want to erase the hell out of this text. You'll never know and I'll be left with a pointless ego and a tortured soul. I'm so selfish. It turns out that I even confess my love to you for my own sake. To make myself feel better.

I just don't understand how? How did this happen? It takes years for people to realise their love. How could I fall in love and change so much in four months? How, Gor?

I don't know what whatever we had between us means to you. But every day I'm convinced that you don't care. As painful as it is for me to realise that, I accept what I see."

"Hi, Milena. I was very surprised by your letter. I don't even know what to answer, where to start. Should I keep silent? You're not hurting me, don't worry. But as for me... I think I've already broken your heart without knowing it. I'm sorry if I gave you hope for nothing. I didn't mean to. I'm not cut out for a relationship, not cut out for a family. You deserve better. Someone to walk down the aisle holding hands with, someone to raise your future children with. And I'm not that man. I live for today, and you think a day ahead. I'll only ruin all your hopes and dreams, which I don't want to do.

As for my pain, there is none. I never have. I don't care. It was just a brief fling. Nothing serious. Forget it. I'm not made for love. Understand. Find your happiness in someone else. Accept it."

"I have realised. I have accepted. Goodbye, Gor."

Not another word.

Cold hands, clenched heart, goose bumps all over my body, lump in my throat, eyes filled with salty liquid. Bump. Pain. A bump. Failure. Impact. Darkness.

She'd expected anything but this reaction. She had expected mutual words, but not contempt. She'd expected a text longer than her own, but not a few vulnerable sentences. She expected a protest at her last words, expected a call, a meeting. Although her brain did not accept the expectation, her heart continued to hope. Deep down she wanted and expected better. She waited for the miracle she had always believed in.

But everything broke. Everything shattered. Her heart beat automatically. She couldn't feel it. There was a hole in her soul as big as her life. She couldn't see, she couldn't hear, she couldn't feel, she couldn't touch. She was in a vegetative state. The lump in her throat grew bigger every day and stopped her breathing.

– You know, I never understood and always condemned Juliet's senseless move when, seeing Romeo dead, she plunged a dagger into her heart. I've never understood the power of love. How can it drive a man to murder? Especially suicide? And now... Astine, I'm in so much pain, so hurt. I don't know how to go on. How to breathe, how to wake up, how to go to bed? Everything has lost its meaning. A man I've only known for four months has made me realise the meaninglessness of twenty–three years of my life.

– Milena, Milena. Wake up, my love. What are you talking about? He's just a boy, Milena. He doesn't deserve you. Don't behave like a teenager. You're smart, beautiful, attractive. You're the best. A thousand boys would do anything for your heart. But you...

– Exactly, Astine. A thousand guys who mean nothing to me would, but the one guy I want not only didn't give me his heart, he took mine. Irrevocably.

– Oh, God, Milena. Don't say that. Please, Milena. It hurts me to look at you. You're not yourself. Forgive me, of course, but I would never have believed that in the twenty–first century such a love could be possible in such a short time. But you're a shining example to me. You're too pure, too emotional and too naive, Milena. You give everything without thinking of the consequences, without thinking of what it will cost you, what price you will have to pay. You gave him what's most precious to you. You gave yourself.

– I know, Astine. I know. I know everything. But I can't help myself. I'm weak. I can't take it, you know?

–No, Milena, no. You're strong. You'll forget him soon. Time will heal everything. Everything will be fine. Trust me.

–I hope so. I really hope so. Otherwise…

Chapter 12

2015. The end of March

The strongest feeling is disappointment...
Not resentment, not jealousy, not even hatred....
There's something left in the soul after disappointment,
but disappointment leaves a void....
— *Erich Maria Remarque*

"Silence. Silence at last."

Milena was sitting on the windowsill of the toilet in the main building. She leaned her head against the glass and stared out of the window. Change. The windows overlooked the university's 'green benches', where all the students spent their free time, except when they were eating lunch in one of the medical centre's three refectories.

After a noisy gynaecology class, Milena had no time to relax. For unknown reasons, she had been suffering from a severe headache all day, and after the noise, not only did the pain get worse, but she also felt nauseous. Usually such subjects as gynaecology were quiet, even too quiet, because the students took them with great interest and seriousness. But for some personal reason, the teacher who gave this lesson was absent, and she was replaced by a very young and inexperienced girl who had not been able to cope with the not–so–interested young people. At the end of the lesson, if you can call it that, Milena told her friends that she had to go down to the university for a minute on some urgent business and that she would meet them as soon as she was done, ran down to the ground floor of the maternity hospital, pushed open the heavy door and stepped outside to go to the university. To be precise, to the main building, where there was always an empty women's washroom on the ground floor. Milena herself did not understand why her feet led her there.

After entering the small room and making sure she was alone, Milena sat down on the half–finished and dusty windowsill with a sigh of relief, not worrying at all about getting her hastily chosen dress dirty.

Some students were walking towards the university buildings, some were standing in groups talking, and some were sitting on benches singing along to the song that always played in the court-yard during the break. Milena could barely hear it through the closed windows, but she could hear her favourite Aerosmith song, 'I don't want to miss a thing', the soundtrack to the film Armageddon. Milena closed her eyes and tried to hear the song. Thoughts swirled in her head. Each of them was fighting for supremacy. But lately there was only one winner. He filled her entire mind, pushing everything else out. He didn't leave her for a moment. It suffocated her from within. It coursed through her entire body, spreading the worst burning pain.

A few minutes later, as Aerosmith replaced Rihanna with 'Di-amonds', Milena opened her eyes. The headache had disappeared without a trace and her mind was clear. Milena started to wipe her eyes, but stopped just in time to avoid ruining her make–up. She took a small mirror from her handbag, looked at it, fixed her hair, smiled artificially at her reflection and put the mirror back in her handbag before heading for the bathroom. Rihanna's voice faded with each step until it was gone as Milena closed the door behind her.

– The concert's in a week and you're singing like you've just picked up a microphone for the first time! – Karina, left alone with Milena, finally managed to speak and raised her voice. – What's wrong with you? It's a happy song about love, about happiness. And you sing it as if you were invited to a wake.

Milena was silent. She could not argue, could not defend herself, could not accept the truth of Karina's words.

– Yes, say something. Don't be so quiet, Milena. What's the matter? What's going on? You and your what's–his–name, remember? Did you have a fight with Gor?

Milena lifted her eyes, in which it was impossible not to feel the pain pouring out in torrents.

A few minutes later, as Aerosmith replaced Rihanna with 'Diamonds', Milena opened her eyes. The headache had disappeared without a trace and her mind was clear. Milena started to wipe her eyes, but stopped just in time to avoid ruining her make–up. She took a small mirror from her handbag, looked at it, fixed her hair, smiled artificially at her reflection and put the mirror back in her handbag before heading for the bathroom. Rihanna's voice faded with each step until it was gone as Milena closed the door behind her.

Milena lifted her eyes, in which it was impossible not to feel the pain pouring out in torrents.

– I know, Karina, I know.

– I feel like a bastard for not being able to help you, but I'll tell you one thing.

Milena looked at her teacher carefully through her tears.

– Use this pain, Milena. Use it where happiness loses its power. Pain can create a masterpiece. Don't let it defeat you. Don't let disappointment bring you down and tie you up. Take the line in your hands. And go for it.

Another concert. Another stage. Another costume.

Milena realised that she couldn't cope with the song Karina had chosen. She had to sing what was closest to her heart. Her lips were silent, but her soul was screaming. She chose Alla Pugacheva's song "I Sing". A song in which she found herself in every line. A song that made her tears flow without stopping.

The hall, as always, was on its feet. But this song brought the audience not only inexplicable emotions. Her heartfelt performance made everyone present share in the pain that had plagued her so much.

She had done what she was striving for. The accumulated negative emotions gave an incomparable fruit – a unique performance.

Chapter 13

2015. April

... The evils of war and the good of peace have been
so well known to mankind that
by men, that ever since we've known men,
the best wish has been the greeting
"Peace be with you".
— Lev Tolstoy

Karabakh.

A geographical region in Eastern Transcaucasia. The name Karabakh is etymologically derived from the Turkish "kara" – black, and the Persian "bah" – garden.

Karabakh covers the area from the Lesser Caucasus Mountains to the plains at the confluence of the Kura and Araks Rivers. It is divided into Plain Karabakh and Nagorno–Karabakh.

From the beginning of the 2nd century BC until the 390s, the territory was within the borders of the Armenian state of Great Armenia of the Artashesid, then Arshakid dynasty, whose north–eastern border, according to Greek–Roman and ancient Armenian historians and geographers, was along the Kura River.

Nagorno–Karabakh was Armenised during its long period as part of Armenia. This process began in late antiquity and was completed in the early Middle Ages – in the VIII–IX centuries. The presence of Artsakh (Karabakh) dialect of Armenian language is reported as early as 700.

Since 1918 Nagorno–Karabakh has been part of Azerbaijan. Nagorno–Karabakh was a disputed territory and the scene of fierce clashes between Azerbaijanis and Armenians until 1920, when it was occupied by the Red Army. By a decision of 5 July 1921, the territory of Nagorno–Karabakh, with an Armenian population of 94%, was incorporated into the Azerbaijani SSR with extensive regional autonomy.

From the second half of 1987, the movement for the transfer of Nagorno–Karabakh from the Azerbaijani SSR to the Armenian SSR became active in the NKAO and in Armenia.

This was followed by a clash between Armenians and Azerbaijanis near Askeran, in which two people were killed. A few days later, a large rally was held in Yerevan calling for the NKAO to be incorporated into Armenia.

From 27 to 29 February 1988, an Armenian pogrom broke out in the town of Sumgait, accompanied by mass violence against the Armenian population, looting, killings, arson and destruction of property, which affected a significant part of the local Armenian population; 26 Armenians and 6 Azerbaijanis were killed, according to official data from the authorities.

Throughout 1988, inter–ethnic clashes between the local Azerbaijani and Armenian populations took place in Nagorno–Karabakh, resulting in the displacement of civilians from their places of permanent residence.

In 1991, the Nagorno–Karabakh Republic (NKR) was proclaimed on the territory of the NKAO and some adjacent Armenian–populated areas. During the 1991–1994 Karabakh war between Azerbaijan and the NKR, the Azerbaijanis gained control of the territory of the former predominantly Armenian Shahumyan district of the Azerbaijani SSR, while the Armenians gained control of the territory of the former NKAO and some adjacent and previously predominantly Azeri and Kurdish areas.

The Defence Army of the Nagorno–Karabakh Republic was officially established on 9 May 1992 as the armed forces of the unrecognised Nagorno–Karabakh Republic, bringing together self–defence units formed in the early 1990s. It consists of motorised infantry, armoured, artillery and anti–aircraft units.

Until the mid–1990s, the Karabakh Self–Defence Army consisted mainly of Karabakh or Azeri Armenians and volunteers from Armenia. At that time, a high percentage of the NKR army's weapons were captured from either Azerbaijani or Soviet forces. A significant amount of weapons and logistics came from Armenia, often at the expense of the regular army. By 1994, the Karabakh Self–Defence Army had established an infrastructure of barracks, training centres and repair bases. The Armenian defeats in Azerbaijan in 1993 were attributed by experts mainly to the self–defence forces, although regular Armenian troops were also involved.

The NKR Defence Army is closely linked to the Armenian armed forces, which provide it with weapons and military equipment. Armenian officers participate in the training of NKR Defence Army personnel, although the Armenian leadership claims that there are no representatives of the Armenian armed forces in and around Nagorno–Karabakh. It is estimated that more than half of the personnel of the NKR Defence Army are residents of Armenia. There is a military unit 33651 of the Armenian army on the territory of Nagorno–Karabakh.

To this day, Armenians who have reached the age of eighteen

serve not only on the territory of Armenia, but also in Nagorno–Karabakh, on the border with Azerbaijan. Thousands of mothers, fathers, sisters, brides have been waiting for their loved ones for two years with fear in their hearts. They hope, they believe, they wait.

Chapter 14

2015. May

A nation unwilling to feed its own army,
will soon be forced to feed another's.
— Napoleon Bonaparte

A shoot–out on the border. Two dead. Five wounded. All soldiers. Young boys. The dead have been identified. The wounded are in hospital. One in serious condition. The families have been informed.

Another tragedy. Another wound. Another pain.

The Abgaryan family received the call at dawn. Her mother's scream was enough for Milena to know that something had happened.

The distance from her room to her parents' room was enough for her to experience all the horror a person could experience. Her heart leapt out of her chest and a lump formed in her throat, choking her. Her limbs shook and she felt dizzy.

When she entered the room, she saw her mother trembling with tears, her father nervously holding a telephone receiver. She rushed to her mother's side, hesitant to ask the question that tormented her.

– Yes, yes. We're on our way. Are you sure your doctors can handle this? OK, OK, OK. I got it. Thank you.

Milena and Sveta looked at Oleg with horrified eyes.

– What are they saying? What's wrong with him? – Sveta could barely contain herself.

– Dad, what's wrong?

– We were lucky, my dears. Everything is fine. Our boy is alive. It's all over now. – Oleg came to his trembling wife and daughter and hugged them tightly. – He's wounded. But it's not serious. He'll be fine. We'd better pack quickly and go and see him. He is in hospital in Stepanakert.

Oleg stood up abruptly and made a beeline for the bathroom. Sveta and Milena could not move. It was as if they were nailed to the bed.

– Oh, God. Oh God, – Sveta repeated.

– Mum, get up, we have to go to Aren's. We haven't a minute to lose.

Milena's inner trembling did not go away. She couldn't believe that all was well. She couldn't believe that fate had been so kind to them. She felt guilty for the families of the dead boys, but happiness for her brother gradually filled her. A heavy stone fell from Milena's shoulders, filling her lungs with oxygen.

Her mother and father came down for coffee. Milena never left her brother's bunk. He'd been shot in the leg. The shin bone was broken. The doctors said the operation was successful.

Milena held her twin's hand. The pain wouldn't let her go. She felt everything he was going through.

"I felt that something was wrong. Milena was incomprehensibly restless that fateful night. All night long she tossed and turned in bed. She couldn't find a place for herself. Something was troubling her heart. But she could not understand what it was. But sitting next to her brother's bed, she understood.

They had felt each other's misfortunes from an early age. Even when they were at a distance, though that rarely happened.

Milena sat up and rested her head on the bed, still holding her brother's hand. Suddenly she felt his hand move. Lifting her head, she met her brother's gentle gaze.

– Hi.

– Hey. How's it going?

– It's terrible to see you like this.

– Yeah, come on. It's OK. – Aren spoke slowly and calmly, but the smile never left his face.

– All right? Fool, you don't know how lucky you are. You could have... – Milena couldn't continue. Just thinking about it made her sick.

– But I'm here, Milena, – Aren said, gripping her sister's hand as tightly as he could.

– Yes, you are here. Thank God you're here.

– Where are Mum and Dad?

– They're downstairs. They've been with you all day. They only came down for coffee a few minutes ago.

– Why aren't you with them? Look at you. You look exhausted.

– Yes, I can see that. You played a big part in putting me in this state.

– I'm sorry, Milena. I didn't mean to scare you. More than anything, I'd hate to see you like this.

– I know, Aren, I know. And I had you in one of them. But it's all right, my love. You'll be back on your feet in a few weeks. You'll be fine. – She ran her free hand gently over his sweaty forehead. – I'm so proud of you. You're my brave, smart boy. I love you so much, Aren. I would give anything for you. Literally anything.

– My twin. I love you so much too. And you have no idea what it means to me to open my eyes and see you holding my hand.

They looked tenderly into each other's tear–filled eyes.

– That's enough. Why did I become so emotional? Must have been the anaesthetic.

A smile on their lips. Hope in their eyes. Love in my heart. Faith in my soul. They're together. They are together again.

A month later, Aren was back on his feet. Every weekend the family visited him in Karabakh. More than once, Milena looked back and realised the horror of what had happened. She could not believe that in the space of a few months she had lived through something she had never dreamed of.

Milena was well aware that what had brought her so much misery was just a drop in the ocean of real cruelty. People go through the worst in their short lives and survive even that.

Milena was spoilt by fate. A golden girl who never faced an obstacle, who did not know the word "no", who got everything she wanted through hard work.

Chapter 15

2015. May

Human beings are born to help one another,
as a hand helps a hand, a foot helps a foot, and the upper
jaw helps the lower jaw.
— Marcus Aurelius

A pleasant cool May evening. A green and strangely empty park. Freshly cut grass, the scent of which filled the whole neighbourhood, and a gentle, refreshing, dancing breeze that carried it further and further, not forgetting to fill the airways of the casual passers–by. The new, clean benches marked 'Yerevan' were empty. Only one bench, in the middle of the park, under a large old oak tree, was occupied by tall, thin girls sitting close together, talking quietly about something. The wind played with their long golden hair.

– Why didn't Ani come? I couldn't reach her, – Milena said, brushing her long, unruly hair out of her face.

– She said she was studying. Ten days before the exam and she's already on tenterhooks.

– Good for her. Not like us. We've forgotten we have finals coming up.

– Oh, come on. Six years of school to worry about an exam you know by heart?

– Yes, you're right.

Milena sat on her side on the bench, leaning on the back of the bench with her left arm and holding her curly hair in the wind with her right hand. Astinee was sitting in the same position opposite her friend, but unlike Milena, she didn't have to hold her hair because the wind was blowing it back into her face.

– Maybe it was for the best that Ani didn't come today.

– Why not? – Astine was surprised.

– I'd like to talk to you.

– About what?

– I want to apologise.

– For what? For what, Milena, I don't understand?

– For everything, Astine. I'm sorry for everything. I'm sorry for dragging you into all the hell that's going on in my life.

– Milena, stop it. Don't you ever say that again.

– But it's true. You're tired of my problems.

– Milena, – Astine said sharply, sitting down next to her friend and taking her cold, soft hands in hers, – look at me.

Milena looked obediently into her friend's beautiful brown eyes.

– If not me, then who? Answer me? – But without waiting for an answer, Astine continued. – If it's not me you need to open your soul to, tell me what makes you happy or tormented, if it's not me you need to cry to, then who? What the hell do you need me for if I'm not there for you on your best and worst days? I love you. You're my partner, my sister, my soul mate. But not like that, of course. Just so Armen doesn't hear.

The friends involuntarily smiled. Astine continued.

– I want to be always at your side. I want to share your sorrows as well as your joys. I want you to share everything with me. I want you to shout, to swear, to laugh your abnormally loud laugh, to shout beside me, to be who you are, to be you. Because that's what you are to me. The closest, the truest, the most faithful, the most loyal, the most unique.

– Astine, my Astine.

Milena hugged her friend tightly, stroking her silky golden hair.

– I love you too. You are an inseparable part of me, and no matter what happens, no matter where fate takes me, no matter what condition I find myself in, you will always be with me. In my heart.

It wasn't long before the friends finally broke the embrace and wiped away the naughty tears.

– Milena, I know I'm repeating myself, but I want you to talk to me. Tell me what's eating you every day. Please talk to me.

– Yes, Astine, you're right. What's going on inside me is in-explicable. It's stronger than me. It's destroying me in small but steady steps. And it's hard for me to deal with it. It's impossible.

– I know he's the problem. That there's only one explanation for your current situation – Gor.

– Yes, you're right, – Milena said, her eyes dropping slightly.

– What do you think of him, Milena?

– It's hard for me to explain, – Milena said after a moment's hesitation.

– Tell me what is in your heart. What you really feel.

Before answering, Milena smiled slightly, which left her friend confused.

– My love for him is like a chronic recurrent aphthous stoma-titis.

– What does that mean? – Astine was still puzzled.

– When he is gone, – Milena continued in a calm voice, – there is a long, peaceful period of remission. There is peace and tranquillity in the soul. But the slightest external stimulus is enough to cause a relapse, with the formation of terribly painful, long–lasting aphthae. And it happens every time. And every time it hurts more and more.

Milena turned her head and wiped away another stream of tears.

– Jesus, Milena, – Astine held her friend in her arms again.

– Astine, answer me, why? What have I done to deserve this? Do I not have the right to mutual love, to happiness? Am I not destined to walk with my lover in the middle, holding hands, to sit with him on a bench in the garden, to embrace him, to kiss him on the neck and receive an answering kiss on the ear? Am I not destined to receive a telephone call and hear, "Yes, darling? "Hello, love." Will I never receive a huge bouquet of white roses, not from another admirer, but from my beloved? And having received them, I will enjoy them until they finally wilt, and I will keep the leaves of the last remaining rose in my favourite book. Will I never answer "I love you" with "I love you too"? Will there never be the one person to whom I will give my heart once and for all? Answer me, Astine! You're my closest friend. You know me better than anyone else. Am I not worthy of all this?

– Oh, Milena, darling. Of course, you are. You deserve the best. You're such a pure, kind person, there's no other way.

– Why then? Why did I get unexpected pain instead of long–awaited love? I didn't need any of it. I didn't want it. I just wanted to love. That's all I wanted. Just love, Astine.

– Sweetheart, cry... Let it all out. Let it all out.

Astine held Milena tightly in her arms. Milena, resting her

head gently on her friend's thin shoulder, continued.

– Astine, why is life like this? I have everything. You know that. Everything a girl dreams of: an excellent, wealthy, loving family, the best friends and girlfriends, an education at the best university, a good voice, a bright future, a nice car, an apartment, mountains of clothes. I can afford to go anywhere, anytime. But I don't have the one thing I've wanted with all my heart all my life. Why is that? There is nothing I dream and pray for more than a strong love for each other. But... .

Milena stopped, unable to continue. The tears had dried on her delicate cheeks and her eyes were slightly swollen.

– Milena, you know. Your whole problem is that you have everything.

Milena lifted her head and looked at her friend in surprise. But she continued without noticing her friend's gaze.

– Those who have no family dream day and night of their parents, of a gentle, normal family life. Those who have financial problems work hard and think about where they can earn more money. Many boys and girls dream of a car, any kind of car, as long as it is made of metal and has four wheels. Many who have never travelled outside their own town dream of at least a little travel, at least within their own country. Milena, you're right. Almost everyone dreams of a life like yours. Believe me, if you didn't have at least one of the things you have, you'd dream about it as greedily as you dream about your other half. It's not your fault, Milena. It's the way humans are made. We don't appreciate what we have. We don't enjoy our surroundings. We often bemoan our own failed, hard lives while living someone else's happy, carefree life. We wait for the future while analysing the past and skipping the present. We get everything wrong. That's why it's always not enough for us.

We want more. But none of us asks the question: maybe enough is enough? Shouldn't we stop what we've achieved and enjoy what we have? Ask yourself this question, Milena. Accept what you already have. And don't chase after what is so far away. When the time comes, it will come to you, without any work, without any effort.

– Thank you.

– For what, Milena? For just saying out loud what you thought and knew better than me.

– Yes, you're right. Thank you for silencing my quiet, impenetrable voice, – Milena said with a smile.

The green park began to fill up with young and old couples, mothers with their children and simply passers–by. Empty benches welcomed all who came. And the warm May breeze continued to play with the golden hair of the two friends.

Chapter 16

2015. June

I did not come to the mosque for a righteous word,
I did not come for the basics.
Last time I stole the prayer rug.
I came for a new one.
— Omar Khayyam

The days passed. For some, they were just torn pages from a calendar; for others, they were fateful decisions and steps. Someone was born, someone died. Life went on with its usual sequence of events. Many things changed and some remained the same.

A painful month passed, during which Milena managed to take the most important step in her life – to pass her final exams and proudly say goodbye to student life. It seemed that she would not be able to do it, that the pain that tormented her would not allow her to do it. But she was stronger. In spite of all the negative inner world, she was able to overcome herself and pass all her exams with distinction. Only she knew the price she had to pay to defeat her most formidable opponent – herself.

Three months had passed since Milena's confession. Three months in which she hadn't spoken to Gor. She'd seen him at the university or on the hospital grounds, but she'd always tried to avoid seeing him. And she almost always succeeded. He didn't show up at the community parties. She knew that was a good thing. She knew that the less she saw him, the sooner things would get better, the sooner she would make a full recovery and he would disappear forever.

The centre of Yerevan. The intersection of Abovyan and Sayat–Nova streets. The Church of St Anna.

It was consecrated on 30 April 2015 by His Holiness Garegin II, Catholicos of All Armenians. The church was part of the complex of the Yerevan residence of the Armenian Catholicos. The construction of the church and the residence began on 30 April 2011 with the financial support of philanthropists Anna and Hrayr Hovnanyan. The project is the work of architect Vahag Movsisyan. According to his idea, the temple of St. Anna will be built next to the XII century chapel of St Katohike, and by its design it will embrace the chapel.

Milena, with a white lace scarf on her head, took small steps towards the altar. Her eyes could not tear themselves away from the beautiful image of the Virgin Mary and the child tenderly cradled in his mother's arms. The church was strangely empty. Not a soul in sight.

"Hello. How are you? I'm fine. I thought I'd come at last. I haven't had time. It's strange, isn't it? I don't know any prayers. I've never even picked up a Bible. I come here and speak to you as an equal. Forgive me for that. But I can't help it. I know you'll hear me, you'll give me the right advice.

I have sinned. No, not in the body. You know that. I have sinned with my soul. I have underestimated and not accepted what You have given me. You did. I was blind. But now I see everything. I see what I have. I see what makes me the happiest person on earth.

And I'm really happy. My family, my friends. They're all alive and well. You saved my brother. I'll thank you for that every day.

I finished university. I'm a dentist now. Can you believe it? Yesterday I walked into a medical school for the first time, and now.... .

Yesterday I started singing in the school play. And now I'm a professional singer with a big future.

Every time I came to Your house, I asked You for one thing, that You put on my path the only one with whom I will spend all my life and to whom I will give this life. But You never granted my wish. And I wanted it so much. I resented You, and I resented You more than once. I didn't understand why. Why did You remain indifferent to my pleas? I blamed you for not listening to me. I complained day after day, not realising how much You really love me. And how grateful I am to You.

Today, for the first time in my life, I have not come to ask You for anything, but to thank You. Thank You for everything.

Thank you for what I have. Thank you for what I have. And thank you for who you are. I accept the life path you have set for me. I will do everything in my power to be worthy. I will heal people, I will sing. I will do what I was born to do. And I will stop chasing the shadows of the past, present and future. Until they themselves come out of hiding and find me.

I smile. I laugh. I laugh at my stupidity, at my blindness. God, I can't believe it. Have I matured? Have I finally realised?

"Thank you. Thank you."

Chapter 17

2015. July

Do no evil, for it will boomerang,
Don't spit in the well, you'll drink the water,
and do not insult those who are beneath you,
if you have to ask for something.
Don't betray your friends, you can't replace them,
and don't lose the ones you love, you can't get them back, don't lie to
yourself –
you'll find out in time
You betray yourself by lying.
— Omar Khayyam

A hot, sunny day in July. Examinations, the ceremony of the Hippocratic Oath, the awarding of diplomas – everything is over. An unknown new world lies in the near future. And in the present... What's in the present? There's so much that defies description. You just have to look around.

An inseparable group of doctors decided to celebrate their graduation from university. There was no better place than Anya's dacha. Everyone had already arrived. Some were already sitting at the big table set up in the garden under the fruit trees, others were walking by the pool, and two of the boys were cooking the main course on the barbecue.

Milena found herself in the kitchen with her friend. They were finishing the last of the preparations. The table was already laid. The only thing missing was the kebab, which the boys outside were still making with great zeal. Ani picked up the cheese plates and headed for the door.

– Milena, I think that's it. Will you do the rest yourself? I'll go and see the guests, OK?

– Yes, Ani, of course. You go ahead. I'll lay this out and be right with you.

Milena was standing at the kitchen table with her back to the door, leisurely arranging the sausage on a plate. The kitchen door opened, but Milena did not turn around, thinking it was Ani who had forgotten something. But whoever it was did not say a word, only the sound of his footsteps slowly approaching. Suddenly Milena felt a breath behind her back, very close. Frightened, she turned round and dropped the sausage she had not had time to put on her plate.

– You scared me, – Milena said, trying to calm herself.

– I'm sorry. I didn't mean to interrupt.

– No, you didn't interrupt, you just scared me. You shouldn't have crept up on me like that.

He was still too close to her. Milena's breathing accelerated. He has to go. He has to leave her alone.

– Gor, did you need something? – Milena asked, trying to pull herself together.

– No. I mean, almost, – Gor said.

– A fork or a knife? – Milena couldn't think of anything.

– Neither, – Gor replied calmly.

– How about a plate?

– No, I don't want that either.

Gor looked her straight in the eye without looking away. Milena, hypnotised by him, stood as if stunned, unable to move.

– Gor, please, if you don't want anything, go away. Let me finish. We're about to sit down to dinner and the appetisers are not yet laid out.

Milena gathered her last strength and turned away, continuing to fold the sausage. But her hands were shaking and would not obey. She had completely forgotten about the piece she had dropped, which was lying on the floor near her foot. Her mind had been taken over by the man's mere appearance. "I thought I was cured. I thought you had left my heart forever."

Gor remained where he was. He didn't move.

– I want to talk, – he said, touching her shoulder lightly.

The touch was enough to make her whole–body shudder, to put her back on the edge.

– I don't think this is a good time to talk, – Milena barely managed to find her voice, – everyone's probably waiting for us. I don't want them spreading rumours about our delay.

Milena struggled to say all this, inside she wanted to hear what he wanted to talk to her about, but her mind wouldn't let her.

– No, now is as good a time as any, – he said firmly.

As if in agreement, they both glanced towards the window, where they could see the table set and their friends engaged in a heated discussion. Neither of them even glanced at the kitchen. Milena realised that she and Gor had a few minutes to wait for the heated conversation to die down.

– Gor, what do you want? What are you up to? It's been so long. I don't think we have anything to talk about.

Taking a cloth from the table and wiping her hands, Milena

turned to face Horus, who was still standing. Their gazes met, but neither turned their heads or lowered their eyes. They continued to stare, filled with feelings that were so different, so distant and yet so identical. Milena felt pain mixed with love. She continued to drown in his eyes that had made her sick for months. The pain in her chest grew with each passing second, burning her heart. The ring finger on her left hand went numb and the numbness gradually crept up her arm. It was hard to breathe.

That was why she was the first to give up. She lowered her eyes and murmured.

– We don't have much time. You wanted to tell me something. I'm waiting.

She could barely get the words out. Her voice was breaking.

– I love you, – Gor said sharply.

Milena looked up at him and the only thing she could manage was a grin.

– What does that mean? – Gor wondered.

Milena could not answer. She just continued to grin strangely.

– Milena, I'm talking to you. What does that look mean? – Gor's voice changed. He was clearly angry.

– It means a good joke, well done. You have a wonderful sense of humour, – Milena replied.

Shudder, muteness, passion, love, pain – the feelings were gone. Everything was taken away, as if by hand. Gor was silent. Milena straightened up. She looked him straight in the eye and said:

– Don't you dare. Do you hear me? Don't you dare. Don't you dare play with my emotions. Don't you dare make fun of me. Don't you dare act like a bastard.

She spoke in a harsh, confident voice, waving her index finger. She wanted to hit him with all her might so that he couldn't say another word. As her hand went to his cheek, he grabbed her wrist. He grabbed her wrist with all his might, so hard that she opened her mouth in sudden pain and moaned.

– Don't you dare raise your hand to me, – Gor's voice was as confident as hers, – I don't know why I've provoked your anger. By confessing? By saying what I should have said long ago? Did I receive a slap in return for a declaration of love?

– A confession? What confession, Gor? That you love me?

Milena ran her free hand over her forehead, as if wiping away sweat that wasn't there. She was cold as ice.

– What's so special about it? What, Milena? Don't I have the right to love you? Don't I have the right to confess? I have no right, damn it? Answer me!

He almost shouted, not noticing that he was squeezing Milena's wrist harder and harder.

– Let go of my hand, you're hurting me. Enough of the moral pain you've put me through.

He released his fingers abruptly, leaving red marks on her wrist. She rubbed her arm with her other hand. She took a few steps away from him and turned towards the window. The friends were still talking. A large plate of kebabs was already on the table. She saw Armen coming to the table and added a new portion of hot meat to the bowl.

– Milena ...

She heard his footsteps approaching.

– Don't come near me. Leave me alone. I don't want to see you, Gor, I don't want to see you anymore, – Milena said, turning to face him.

– Milena, I love you. Honestly, I love you.

Even noticing the distrust in Milena's eyes, Gor continued.

– Listen to me, please. Just hear me out.

Milena replied with silence.

– I was wrong, – Gor began calmly, – so you misunderstood my attitude towards you. I liked you at first sight. But at that moment I didn't pay attention to it. I woke up the morning after we met and while I realised that you had completely absorbed my thoughts, I was already sending you a friend request on Facebook. I wrote to you every day, anxiously awaiting your reply. Corresponding with you every day brought me immense energy and stimulation. I didn't notice all this until one day I realised that I was in love, – Gor said the last words slowly, emphasising each word. And when he said the last word, he lowered his gaze, as if embarrassed by his feelings. – I'm sorry. I was unfair to you. I was just scared. Scared of my feelings for you. I was afraid to fall in love again, to let someone into my life again, to... Oh, shit." Gor's voice trailed off. He clutched his head with his hands, looking up at the ceiling. "Yes, damn it," he continued suddenly, lowering his hands and looking Milena straight in the eyes, "yes, I was afraid. You didn't show your feelings at first. I couldn't imagine that you reciprocated me. So, I tried to ignore you. Ignore you, pretend you were some insensitive alphonso. And when you confessed to me, I was so confused. I couldn't believe my eyes. I couldn't believe that my feelings for you were mutual. I didn't want to hurt you. That's why I backed off. I thought that if I was away, you would soon forget me, like so many others have done. But all the time I was watching you. And you just walked by with indifference. I thought I was doing the right thing by not opening my heart to you. But things changed. I changed. But my feelings for you stayed the same. I finally lifted the veil that covered my eyes. I saw what I should have seen a long time ago. I realised how much I needed you. I couldn't live in a world without you. Believe me, Milena, believe me. I wouldn't joke with you like that. I wouldn't. I know how you feel. I know you love me too. You still do. I know you do. I can see it. I can see it in your eyes.

Milena, listening in silence, ran her hand down his unshaven cheek. With every movement, the stubble digging into the dermis pricked her delicate fingers. But she didn't let go of his hand.

– I loved you. I loved you so much. But that love brought me nothing but pain, resentment, humiliation. Nothing at all.

Milena spoke in a calm, quiet voice, still holding her hands up and looking into his eyes.

–You didn't see me. You didn't notice. You saw everyone but me. You had fun with anyone who gave you the slightest excuse. You never missed an opportunity. During those three months apart, whenever we met by chance, you were always accompanied by a girl. You were always smiling and looking happy. And after all this, you want me to believe your feelings? After your reaction to my confession, do you want me to believe that you were in love with me all along and just kept quiet? I'm sorry, but your words are far from the truth.

Milena finally lowered her hand, quickly wiping away the tear that had just rolled down her cheek.

– I repent that I was wrong. Milena, I repent. – Gor looked at her with pleading eyes. – Milena... I've never apologised to anyone before. You're the only one I'm like this with.

– You didn't even know how much I loved you all this time, – Milena continued without hearing his words, – didn't know how much I suffered when I saw you with another companion. I didn't know how I waited with bated breath for our next meeting. How I memorised every word you said, every move you made, every action you took. You were everything to me, Gor. Everything. I got up in the morning and went to bed at night thinking only of you.

– You didn't tell me anything. How could I have known? How could I have known you loved me? If I had known before, things would have been different.

Milena smiled slightly.

– All you had to do was look at me and into my eyes and you would have known. But you didn't. And when I did, you disappeared, – she said quietly.

– You could have at least given me a clue. I'm not Nostradamus, am I?

– Yes, you're right. I could have. I thought I'd regret it, that I'd never get over it. I'm such a weakling with a useless ego. I made the biggest mistake of my life that day when you found out how I felt. I haven't been able to forgive myself since.

– No, you're not weak, don't say that.

– Yes, Gor, I am. You found out how I felt. And when you did, you gave me an answer I'll never forget. It was the greatest blow to my ego. You have no idea what I've been through. All because of you, Gor, because of you. I felt low, fallen.

– Milena, stop, what are you talking about? You just loved. You loved, Milena. You didn't do anything wrong, you just loved. Your love is as pure as my love for you. You are pure, Milena. You are the clearest and kindest person I know, – Gor said, lowering his voice a little.

– Yes, I have loved, Gor. I had the chance to love you. You, Gor. But you didn't deserve my love, you didn't. And you still don't. – Milena didn't change her calm tone.

– Milena, I have realised my mistake. I love you. Damn it, what else can I say to make you believe me? How can I prove it to you? – said Gor, not taking his pleading eyes off her.

– Keep your voice down or they'll hear you outside and I don't want them to, – she said in a whisper.

– I don't care about anyone. I'm only interested in you right now. I only care about your opinion, your answer, – he said in the same raised voice.

Milena smiled again. A paradox. A defence. She couldn't believe her ears, couldn't believe that what she was hearing was coming from the man she most wanted to hear it from, but least expected it from.

– It's strange. You used to only care about me and other people's opinions. It's a strange life, isn't it, Gor? Once I would have given anything for this day, for this conversation, for this moment. And when it came, I didn't care. Now I don't care.

She ran her hand gently down his cheek again, then through his hair. And she went on, as hard as it was for her to say it all, she went on.

– I don't love you anymore, Gor. Not one bit. I fell out of love with you the day I confessed it to you. If I had known that my confession would free me from you, from this feeling, from all this suffering, I would have done it from the first time we met.

– No, I don't believe you, – Gor said, shaking his head.

– You have to believe. You have to accept reality. It's over, Gor. It's over before it even started. I've had enough of you. It's been too long. I've lost too much because of you. But I'm cured. The important thing, Gor, is that I'm healthy now. So my advice to you is to stay out of it, so you don't get it yourself. Live your life. Create a new life that doesn't include the stupid fool who managed to love you so much.

– No, Milena, no. I won't just let you go. No. You're too precious to me to let go so easily. I don't believe your love is gone, I don't believe it. True, strong love never goes away. Never, Milena.

Milena listened to his words and realised that they were true.

– I love you, Gor. I love you to this day. I love you even when I hate you. But you won't know that. No one else will ever, ever know. I'll be your past. And you will always be my present and my future.

– Gor, don't, there's nothing more you can do. Let's stop this pointless conversation.

– Milena...

Their conversation was interrupted by Armen's voice from outside.

– All right, everybody to the table, – Armen said, putting the last pieces of meat into the bowl with the kebab.

– Where's Milena? – Ani said, looking out the kitchen window, – she should have finished by now.

– And where is Gor? – asked Armen.

– I'll go and have a look, – said Ani and went into the kitchen.

Surprised, Gor and Milena turned away from each other. Milena had barely picked up the plates of snacks when the kitchen door opened and Ani walked in.

– Are you here too? – asked Ani, probably surprised to see Gor. Ani immediately shifted her gaze from Gor to Milena without getting an answer from him. – Milena, what took you so long? Did something happen? I was so busy talking to the boys that I forgot that I left you in the kitchen.

– No, Ani, no, it's fine. I was just trying to arrange the appetisers more carefully. And Gor just came in for a drink of water, – Milena excused herself.

Ani looked at Gor who was standing by the window without a glass in his hand. She didn't believe them. They were too suspicious.

– Come on, let's go, they're all waiting, – Ani finally said.

They all went to the exit together. Ani went out first, followed by Milena with plates in her hands, and Gor came out last, closing the kitchen door behind him.

The day went well as usual. Fun company. Real friends. Jokes, laughter. Memories, joy. Delicious food. Music. Alcohol.

Throughout the day, Ani and Astine kept a close eye on Milena so that no one would notice. After the incident in the kitchen, Ani was reluctant to share her concerns with Astine. They noticed how Milena changed throughout the day. She would be happy or sad, smiling or almost crying. But no one noticed except her two close friends. Although...

The pair of black eyes never managed to settle down and enjoy the company of friends. The pair of black eyes had been wandering all day, searching, hoping to catch a glimpse of beautiful, kind brown eyes. But all day long they never succeeded. Not even once.

Epilogue

2015. August

Isn't it ridiculous to save a penny a century?
When you can't buy eternal life?
This life has been given to you, my darling, for a while, —
Try not to miss the time!
— Omar Khayyam

"Hello, my darling. How are you? How are you? How's your food? Have you eaten? Not hungry? You know, today is exactly one year and two months since you left. Only ten more months and we'll be together again. I miss you so much. Mum and Dad are coming to see you in September. I don't know if I can go with them. It depends on my next tour.

Yes, by the way. I have a gig in a week. I've been preparing for it for so long. I've worked so hard. I hope I can live up to all my hard work and Karina's hard work.

I had a lot of doubts about which song to choose. I couldn't decide. Just recently I chose Larisa Dolina's song "Don't Need Words". My heart was telling me to choose this song. A strange choice, I know. I'm not quite sure myself. But my heart is telling me yes. I want to take the risk. I know you'll support me no matter what. From the first notes of this song, I'm in it and she's in me.

I'm sorry you won't be at the concert. I would have loved it more than anything. But, you know, the thought that you are there, where every Armenian should spend two years of his life, that you survived a terrible shooting, gives me a lot of strength. I'm so proud of you. You are so good, so smart. My brother, my close friend. My blood.

You know, I've changed. You'll notice it when you get here. So many things have changed in your absence. Although we've seen each other recently, the last time was too much for both of us.

But let's not talk about it. I don't want to burden you with bad memories and unnecessary information. Just know this: I'm fine, I'm great. Your twin is happy, which means you're happy. I can feel it. I know it.

Write to me more often. Describe life in the army in great detail. I'm terribly interested. I want to be a part of you, even at this distance.

You know, Aren, I pray for you every day, for all our boys on the border. Stay safe, live and come back.

I love you very, very much. Miss you, kisses, hugs."

It was the end of August. The most important day in the life of Milena, the girl who sings, was approaching. The song was ready. The dress for the evening was ready. Only her heart was beating unaccustomedly, as she was about to embark on a new life and new heights.

A huge stage. The warmth of burning multi–coloured spot-lights. A group of musicians in the right–hand corner of the stage. Three beautiful background singers in the left corner.

Suddenly all the spotlights went out. Only one remained on, illuminating a tall, thin girl standing in the middle of the stage, her golden hair pulled back into a beautiful bun, wearing a long, tight red dress with a plunging neckline. A microphone in her right hand. The gaze of intense sparkling eyes.

Music... Voice... Feelings... Emotions... Adrenaline... Love... Happiness... Life... .

With each note, the stage gradually lit up and filled with a special warmth and cosiness.

As the music faded, Milena lowered her head. A second later, the explosion of applause drowned out even her inner voice. Tears involuntarily trickled down her cheeks. She raised her head. The hall was on its feet. The admiring glances of the audience, the endless rapturous shouts turned her inner world upside down. Her eyes cried, but her soul rejoiced. The pain that had suffocated her for so many months left her with the last notes of the song. She opened her soul, shared what had tormented her, and it saved her.

She let go of the past and thought nothing of the future. She marvelled at what she had at that moment. Milena wanted as much as possible to see everyone present, all those who were so happy about her success. Parents, girlfriends, friends – everyone was in the audience. Everyone was applauding, everyone was admiring.

She saw so many shining eyes looking at her, but she never noticed a pair of black eyes full of hope. Eyes that were screaming, fighting for a look back. Eyes filled with so much love that they wouldn't give up under any circumstances. Eyes that would sparkle at the sound of that voice, that would hope and fight and believe to the end.

Forever.

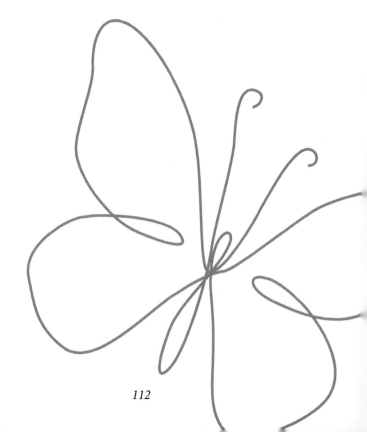

AND A BUTTERFLY SOARED

And A Butterfly Soared

The caterpillar never became a butterfly if it clung to the past.

Anyway...

What do we all want in this life? Why do we wake up every morning, get out of bed, study, work, earn, spend, study again, travel, love, kiss, marry, divorce, have children, go to parties, drink, eat, listen to music, dance, walk, play sports, dress, undress, have sex, go back to the same bed at night (or maybe to another bed) and fall asleep with hope for tomorrow? What's the point of all this? What's the point of this whole cycle of events? What are the goals, the dreams, the hopes, if the end is the same?

There are a lot of questions. And there's almost no answer. And you don't need one.

Only by living life and doing all this do you realise that it is not all in vain. Every little thing is not in vain. Sometimes we find in it what every human being on this planet, consciously or not so consciously, is looking for – happiness.

One day she was handed a piece of paper with the words: "What do you think happiness is?"

She was a little confused. She handed back the blank sheet. She thought about it.

Prologue

Yerevan, 2020. Summer

The air filled her lungs with peace and lightness. She sat on the freshly cut grass, filling every second, every breath and every breeze with happiness.

She smiled. It was a real, genuine smile that she had missed for so long.

The laughter of her two– year– old twins playing happily near-by. The May sun gently warming her golden skin.

She felt the warmth of a man's palms on her shoulders. She didn't even look back. The goose bumps all over her body made her aware of the identity of the man standing behind her. Still keeping her eyes on the little princesses, she covered his hands with her delicate arms. A moment later, her husband's arms were around her. She smiled again. He sat down beside her, continuing to embrace his wife.

She looked into his love– filled eyes. A pair of black eyes shone. Their lips met in a passionate, though not long, kiss.

– I love you, Milena.

– And I you.

Goosebumps continued to move across her golden skin. She'd heard those words a thousand times, said them a thousand times herself. But each time they were more confident and sincerer, and each time they left their magical effect.

He hugged her even tighter. Looked into the clear, happy brown eyes. Her lips curved into a smile, her eyes sparkled.

– Thank you for everything, Milena.

She looked into his coal– black eyes in amazement. Her heart froze in anticipation. It didn't take him long.

– Thank you for the fact that despite the problems and greyness of the world around me, I see all its bright colours and charms. Thank you for these two angels who look just like you. Thank you for making me appreciate this life.

She said nothing. His words touched her fragile broken heart. She felt another shard being repaired. She ran her right hand gently down his freshly shaved cheek and kissed him again. Laying her head on his shoulder, she looked at the children.

"I'm the one who should be thanking you for everything. I'm the one who should appreciate every wound you've healed. And I am grateful. I'm happy."

She was sure that some time later all the wounds would heal. The pieces of her heart would be put back together, allowing her to breathe again.

He loved her. She loved him. He never judged her, but accepted her with all her flaws and idiosyncrasies.

But the hardest part for her was to forgive herself, to forget the past and accept the present in all its glory.

Chapter 1

Yerevan, 2015. End of September

"Hello, my dear Astine. I'm writing to you and I realised that our letters and conversations are becoming less frequent. I don't blame you. I know that many things have changed for you since you left for St. Petersburg. Your husband, your job. I miss you so much. I really need you. But I shouldn't be selfish. You're happy. You've achieved everything you ever wanted.

But...

You left inopportunely. And I stayed inopportunely.

I have so much to tell you. I know you'll be surprised when you see my letter. But I can't say it all on the phone. I have to write it all down. Please read it when you have time. You don't have to answer, it doesn't matter. It's just important that you know.

He came back into my life. Right after you left. Not even a month ago. A lot has changed. You have no idea how much.

I was so lonely. I missed you so much. You were far away. I was short of breath.

I went to the first hospital to do a residency in family dentistry, just like I was supposed to. Where Gor worked.

You see, the meeting was inevitable. We met by chance, to be honest, in the hospital canteen. I walked by without noticing. He tried not to notice me.

But my hands were shaking. I quickly headed to my table to

put down my tray of food. My inner trembling made it impossible for me to hold it.

He was sitting at the next table. Neither of us touched our food. Astine, I didn't think that a meeting could rekindle the fire that I had so carefully extinguished. But now I know. The fire never went out. I just moved a decent distance away so I couldn't see him. And it was burning all the time.

You must be surprised. It's been almost a month. I haven't mentioned any of this to you.

I thought I'd give you the good news right away. Either that I'd dumped him and gotten rid of him once and for all, or that we were finally together. Yes, I know, I'm stupid. But as soon as I saw him I knew I was ready to forgive him more than once and I was ready to let him into my life more than once.

I didn't want to upset you. I didn't want to disappoint you. It's hard for me to find the right words. It's hard to speak from the heart. I have so many emotions inside me.

After our accidental meeting, it was on to the not– so– accidental ones. I honestly tried my best not to fall into that net again. I ran away from him. From my feelings. But they were much stronger. Much stronger.

As I write all this down, I wonder if time could go back and knowing how things would turn out, would I have warned myself of all this? Would I have closed the doors of my heart and my life?

What scares me is that I don't have a clear answer to that question. And I don't think I ever will.

I picked up my phone, clutching it tightly as the screen lit up with his number. My heart began to beat faster, my eyes sparkled, my soul filled with happiness and contentment. And so it was with every call, every text message.

Did that make you smile? I know I'm like a child. But he's the only one who makes me that child. He makes me like no one has ever seen me before. Probably only my parents in childhood, when I was sincerely happy about a new Barbie doll or some incomprehensible trinket.

I wake up and go to bed with a smile on my face. Looking in the mirror, I just don't recognise myself. My eyes are on fire, Astine. There's fire in my eyes.

Whatever I wear, whatever hair and make– up I choose, I like it all. I always feel comfortable.

I walk down the street smiling. Always friendly, kind. Nothing can spoil my mood. Even if there are problems with the patients, I find a solution quickly and effortlessly. I don't get nervous, I don't get angry, I don't criticise. All negative emotions are out of my system. I am full of love. It's in every cell of my body. Astine, it's unbelievable. How can one person, just by being in my life, change both my inner and outer worlds?

There are a lot of questions and almost no answers. So, I try not to ask too many questions any more. It's all strange to me. All these feelings and emotions are foreign to me. And, I won't lie, I'm scared. I'm like a deaf person who has heard a sound for the first time and is able to say the word.

Yes, I'm scared. But I like it all. I want to try it. Even if it hits me at the end, I'm willing to risk it.

Well, my dear, wait for my letters. I hope they will always be joyful and positive.

Love you very much.

Sent.

Chapter 2

September, 2015

The passion was stronger. She couldn't just look at him, look away and continue to sit quietly. Each time, her body filled with emotion, her lower abdomen burning. Not even the witnesses sitting next to her became a barrier. She wanted him with her whole being, her whole body, her whole soul.

She looked into his black eyes that sparkled when he spoke, then at his indirect, slightly crooked nose, the stubble so handsome and masculine. His lips. He laughed, revealing his not– so– white teeth.

She watched every movement of the lip muscles, every slight twitch. In her mind, she kissed and bit them, and they returned the kiss. In thought, in a passionate kiss, their tongues twirled in a disorderly dance. Her eyes gradually moved down his manly neck. Left ear. The storm of memories caused Milena to look away. "I can't do this anymore. I can't hold myself back. What are you doing to me?"

– Milena, tell me you agree with me.

– What?

Milena looked at her friend in surprise, expecting her to remind her what she was talking about. But Ani did not perceive her friend's worried look.

– I'm sorry. I didn't hear what she said. I was lost in my own thoughts. – Milena said sincerely, finding no support in her friend.

By chance, Milena caught sight of Gor, who had a grin on his face.

– Stop smiling. – Milena said laughing and pushed Gor aside.

After meeting their friends, they went out to walk around and enjoy the warm autumn evening.

– Sorry, sorry. – Gor said, also laughing. – I can't get the look on your face out of my head. What were you so busy with? Me, I hope?

– Don't even think about it said Milena, laughing.

– Well, now I'm pretty sure you were thinking about me, – said Gor, looking at Milena with sparkling black eyes.

Their eyes met. They both smiled embarrassedly. Gor was changing before their eyes. Milena had never noticed the confusion in his masculine, smug, sometimes cynical eyes. She realised that their interactions were changing him day by day. He becomes more romantic, more tender, more attentive. Although very often he did his best to hide his feelings and not to appear in such a light to Milena, because he thought that this would reveal his weakness, which was unacceptable for a man like him.

But Milena was no fool. She understood everything very well. And very often she played along with him, not wanting to hurt his inflated male pride and self– esteem.

– You're so cocky, Aznavuryan. Milena often called Gor by his surname.

Gor took her by the waist and turned her to face him. Hugging her tightly, he sizzled her with his gaze. Milena's whole body trembled, swallowing her saliva with difficulty. Gor smiled again.

– Stop smiling and playing with my nerves. – said Milena trying to get out of his embrace.

But Gor held her too tightly, not for a moment thinking of letting go.

– Where are you going?" he said, squeezing her even tighter in his embrace.

– Let go. You're choking me.

Milena's words didn't match her wishes. The last thing she wanted was for him to let her go. If it were up to her, she would stay in his arms forever.

– I will never let you go. – Gor said, gently kissing the tip of her nose.

– Your words give me goose bumps all over my body.

– Me too. – said Gor, kissing Milena again. – I never thought that I would embrace a girl like this and kiss her in the middle of the day in front of everyone.

Milena smiled. Her eyes burned. Her heart was beating fast. She felt boundless true happiness. She wanted to capture this moment forever. Mentally she photographed every moment, saving each photo in the depths of her heart.

– You know, one of my friends says that nothing lasts forever. Everything ends sooner or later. The good and the bad. That's why she doesn't have the word "forever" in her vocabulary. I'm afraid of that word too, Gor. Just like I'm afraid of our happiness. It's too good to be true.

– Have you lost your mind again, silly girl? – said Gor, smiling, looking at Milena and hugging her tightly. – Where are all these thoughts coming from? Don't you dare think of such things. Do you understand, Milena?

Milena nodded obediently.

– I can't hear you. Do you understand me?

Yes, – Milena replied, nuzzling his neck and breathing in the scent of his favourite body.

– How about a mug of cold beer? – Gor suddenly asked.

– With great pleasure. – Milena answered without raising her head.

Many breweries have opened in Yerevan over the past few years, each trying to attract visitors in its own way. And indeed, each was special in its own way. But you could get your fill of tasty beer and unique snacks at any of them.

Gor and Milena chose the brewery at the intersection of Abovyan and Pushkin streets. The three– storey building was always crowded with visitors.

On the third floor there was a square terrace surrounded by low ornamental plants, from which they could see the elite buildings of the Northern Avenue.

One wall was completely taken up by a bar, behind which a handsome young barman was polishing beer mugs with a small cloth in his right hand. Numerous tables and comfortable sofas filled the rest of the room. Quiet music played in the background. There were a few visitors. The brewery was filling up towards the evening. The atmosphere was relaxed and calming.

After a couple of glasses of dark beer, Milena settled down like a kitten next to Gor, covering herself with the warm blanket the waiter offered.

– I just want to drink with you. – Milena said suddenly.

– Why is that? You and your friends aren't too bad. – Gor said and kissed her on the head.

– Yes. – Yes, I do. But, you know, just drinking makes me vulnerable, too honest. And that's the kind of person I only want to be with you. You're the only one I trust.

Gor didn't say anything. He only thought, holding Milena even closer to him.

– I love you, Gor. And I always want to be close to you, under your strong and reliable wing, Milena said, cuddling closer to her lover.

Every day they spent together was special and memorable. On days when Gor was on duty, Milena visited him in the evening, if only for a few minutes. The many calls from the reception prevented them from being together for longer. She always brought Gor's favourite burgers and a Coke. Sitting in the hospital garden, Gor handled them with great gusto.

Milena and Gor's colleagues never stopped watching the young couple with curiosity. For the first month of their relationship, Milena and Gor were the talk of the town. They were a beautiful and enviable couple.

Absorbed in love and each other, they did not notice anyone around them and avoided all rumours and unnecessary talk.

Chapter 3

October, 2015

A torn calendar sheet. Another one.

One day older. One day wiser. A day more conscious. Or maybe quite the opposite.

Milena sat down at her small table. Looked at her reflection in the little mirror on the table. A beautiful oval face. Big brown eyes, long thick eyelashes, not very wide eyebrows making the look piercing and unforgettable, pronounced cheekbones, small nose, symmetrical but not very plump lips. Long wavy golden hair fell down over her chest, reaching her waist.

Milena ran her long, delicate fingers through her hair, never stopping to look at her reflection. She wasn't thinking about anything. Her gaze froze in her burning eyes. She was young, beautiful, energetic, intelligent, educated and now loved.

It seemed to her that no one and nothing could extinguish the light in her eyes, which had been lit with such difficulty. But they continued to burn with a real, bright, terrible flame. She smiled. She was frightened.

"I don't believe any of this is real. I don't believe it's really happening. It's too good to be true. I love him, Astine. Stronger every time I see him. Without him, I'm short of breath, but I smile. As soon as I think of him, of us, and I think of it all the time, I smile. Happiness fills me.

I'm scared.

I've never felt this good. I've never felt so completely happy.

What is it?

I won't think about anything. I'll just savour every moment in silence.

You just wished me a happy birthday and I'm back ......".

Milena was slowly climbing the stairs when she heard the voices of several girls behind her. The voices approached quickly. Milena stopped and wanted to move, giving way to those who were coming up, when she saw the familiar faces of her classmates. Among the five cheerful faces, she immediately spotted a snow–white skinned one with black shining eyes.

– Hello, Milena.

Milena, who had been standing stoically without moving from her seat, came to her senses as soon as she heard the voice.

– Oh, hey, guys. It's good to see you. What brings you here?

Everyone else said hello to Milena, too.

– We've come to borrow books from a doctor. – We're here. – Izyuminka answered for everyone.

– All together again. – said Milena, smiling.

The girls also smiled and looked at each other happily.

– Oh, Milena, it's already becoming a tradition for us to meet on our birthday. – said Maria, walking up to Milena. – Congratulations, beauty.

– Congratulations, Maria.

The girls hugged each other gently. The others congratulated Milena. Suddenly Maria put her left hand on Milena's head. Milena looked surprised at first, but when she understood her classmate's gesture, she smiled even wider.

– Thank you very much.

– You deserve it, Milena. – said Maria, her eyes burning with a real fire of happiness. – Believe me, the best thing that can happen to a girl is to become the wife of the man she loves. It is the greatest gift in life. I wish it for you with all my heart.

Milena, excited by Maria's words, hugged her tightly. – Thank you, darling. Thank you so much.

Maria just smiled.

– Well, we'll be off, because we've got a lot to do today, and so do you, I think. Have a good time.

– Thank you, girls. – Thank you. Kisses, everybody.

– And you. – said Izyuminka from the top of the stairs.

When the former classmates disappeared on the first floor, some incomprehensible feelings seized Milena. Maria's black sparkling eyes could not get out of her head. Milena, just by looking at them, realised that she was infinitely sincerely happy. In the morning Milena saw her own light in her reflection. But the latter was not the same. Milena was left with an uncomfortable feeling. It prevented her from fully enjoying the gifts of fate.

She realised that Aren was far away from everyone else to celebrate the day. Their shared day. But the thought that her brother was perfectly fine was comforting to Milena. And a grand party awaited her in the evening with friends, colleagues, family, and most importantly, Gor.

The thought of Gor made Milena's heart race. She smiled involuntarily. A warmth ran through her body, her heart fluttered, her lips smiled and her eyes sparkled with real fire.

Remembering the latter, Milena's heart raced. She smiled involuntarily. Her body felt warm, her heart fluttered, her lips smiled, and her eyes sparkled with genuine fire.

She was about to introduce him officially to the attendees and especially to his parents.

Milena knew they would like Gor. He had all the qualities any parents would want in their daughter's future husband. Especially that Milena had never been so happy before. And the latter could not escape the attentive and loving parents.

At seven in the evening the guests began to gather at a restaurant in the capital. Milena, dressed in a scarlet knitted dress with flared sleeves, round neckline, raw edges, above the knees in the front, and a relatively long train in the back, greeted the guests with a genuine smile, but with a special excitement, periodically fixing her golden wavy loose hair falling down to her shoulders.

By half past eight, all but one had gathered. The sparkle in Milena's eyes began to fade.

She glanced at her phone, then at the front door. Milena tried her best to pull herself together, to join in the fun, but her inner resentment was stronger. She ran through all the possible reasons for his absence. But nothing came to mind because he had promised to come. She felt that something was wrong.

Milena noticed the stern look on her father's face. He was obviously displeased with her confusion. The guests celebrated and drank to their health. They reminisced about Aren. Milena forced a smile so as not to make her father even angrier.

The musicians arrived at eight o'clock in the evening. A real party began. To the hit song of Armenchik, a famous Armenian singer, Milena's guests filled the dance floor one by one. Milena followed their movements in the rhythm of the music, but her thoughts were far away.

Suddenly, the screen of her smartphone lit up. Milena looked sharply at the phone and excitedly picked it up, bringing it close to her face. Her heart raced.

"My dear, forgive me for not keeping my promise and not coming. I had to do my duty as a doctor. A number of injured people had been brought to the hospital as a result of the accident. We were called immediately. We needed a full trauma team. Just finished one surgery. I'm about to do another.

I don't know when I'll be finished. I don't want to make any false promises.

But believe me, I'll do my best to see you tonight so I can kiss you before midnight.

I kiss you. And a big hug.

Have fun.

A veil of sadness covered Milena's beautiful face. She texted, "Thanks. Good luck," and put the phone down on the table. Her eyes fell on the crowd, who were having a great time, dancing to the rhythm of Armenian music. Today was her day. Everyone had gathered for her and was celebrating her day. But she couldn't gather herself to join her guests.

– Come on, get up to dance, I'm getting angry. – Milena was surprised to hear her father's voice in her left ear.

– Yes, Dad, of course. I was just about to dance. – said Milena, standing up from her seat.

She did her best to hide her eyes from her father, so that he wouldn't notice her sadness. But she was a poor actress. She was unable to hide her negative emotions and her bad mood.

Despite the circumstances, the evening was a success. After talking to her brother, Milena's mood improved noticeably, after which she drank a couple of glasses of wine and started dancing and having fun. And at ten o'clock in the evening, Milena blew out the candles of a two– storey ombré cake and made a wish.

It was around eleven o'clock in the evening when the restaurant manager approached Milena, asking her to sing a song. Milena didn't agree immediately, but with the support of the people around her, she went on stage.

Absorbed in the conversation with the musicians and the choice of song, Milena didn't notice when the front door opened and a new visitor entered the hall. Noticing the familiar faces, he approached the table. He was greeted and sat down in the seat originally reserved for him. Ani pointed him towards the stage. His coal– black eyes lit up as they always did when he heard her voice.

Music filled space. Milena, standing in front of the microphone, closed her eyes. They were filled with every note, every word of her performance. The dance floor quickly filled with couples.

Milena opened her eyes, looked at her table continuing to sing. Suddenly she saw him. Their eyes met. He stood up. She smiled, her skin covered with goose bumps, her eyes sparkled and filled with tears. The song took on a completely different aura, within seconds it became sincere.

Milena couldn't hide her inner trembling. He slowly approached the stage. The song had ended. The dancing couples stopped. Loud applause drowned out everything around her. But Milena saw nothing, heard nothing. He reached out his hand and helped her down from the stage.

– You've come," she said, running her hand over his soft cheek and looking at his tired eyes.

– Yes. I promised. – He replied, kissing her gently on the forehead.

They held each other's hands and looked tenderly at each other, hesitant to take the next step. They were like two teenagers on a first date who, having tasted love for the first time, were shy of it.

– I have a present for you, but it's in the car. – I don't want to give it in front of witnesses. I don't want to give it in front of witnesses.

Milena's heart fluttered. She had received quite a few gifts today, but the one she was to receive from him was the most desirable, even without knowing what exactly he had prepared for her.

Despite all the witnesses, including her parents, she hugged Gor tightly. He embraced her with a particular embarrassment, but real passion.

– I'm embarrassed. – said Gor and continued to hug Milena.

Milena let go of him and laughed.

– Gor, what's wrong with you? I never thought you could be so embarrassed.

– Believe me, I didn't know much about myself before I met you.

Their passionate gazes continued to absorb each other. But they had to pull away as their friends approached. Milena looked over to the table where her parents were sitting, watching their daughter with a smile on their faces. Meeting the eyes of her parents, Milena smiled.

It was a moment Milena would never forget. This image was deeply engraved in her memory. Just one look was enough to understand and accept her parents' blessing.

It is a wonderful feeling for every girl to know that her parents accept her choice. This is probably the most important stage in any relationship.

Milena couldn't sleep that night. Her heart kept pounding. Lying on her side, she kept looking at the photos from the evening. She enlarged the photos of herself and Gor, scrutinising every detail.

Gor went back to the hospital after the restaurant. But Milena couldn't sleep without writing to him.

"Thank you for coming. Thank you for being there. My whole family was there for me, but I felt an unpleasant emptiness. With you here it all made sense.

Have a good shift, love. I can't wait to see you in the morning.

P.S. Thanks for the gift, Gor. It's beautiful.

When Milena finally fell asleep, she was clutching the necklace and pendant – a butterfly – that Gor had given her.

Chapter 4

November, 2015

"Astine, you won't believe this, but I was oblivious to everyone around me. Everything was burning inside. I understood the undeniable truth – relatives, friends – all those who are always by my side, in any situation, at any problem and turmoil, I was ready to leave these people, to exchange their company, meeting with them for a date with him. Wherever I was, whatever I was busy with, I cancelled and left everything to meet him.

A phone call from him, a look, a touch, a kiss or just his presence and everything is fine. There are no more problems of any kind. Life is beautiful".

He confidently opened the window, climbing into her room. She got out of bed, slightly startled.

– Silly. You could have fallen.

– Never.

They approached each other. With one hand he took her waist and pulled her to him; with the other he took her chin and guided her delicate face to his. She closed her eyes as she tasted his lips. Her hands moved to his head. Long fingers sank into his short–cropped hair. The slow calm kiss gradually turned into a passionate fusion of lips. His tongue sank into her mouth. And she drowned in his embrace.

They walked slowly towards her bed. She sat on the edge, he

remained standing, bent over but not parting their lips. Gently, lightly, he took her in his arms and placed her on the bed, lying down beside her. His lips and tongue, releasing her lips, travelled down her neck. She opened her mouth slightly and moaned. Goosebumps ran down her body, the bottom of her stomach burning. He tried to pull down the strap of her nightdress, but she grabbed his hand. But he proved more persistent and his desire stronger. Without stopping to caress her, he eagerly but still pulled the straps down, exposing her delicate white cleavage. Milena felt everything burn inside her – a new, strange, painfully pleasant. But no matter how hard she tried, her brain wouldn't shut down and she couldn't relax and enjoy it.

– Stop it. Please stop.

Pushing him away, she got up and went to the window. From the window, through the darkness, she could see the small garden, the neighbouring houses. The lanterns were not lit. It was well past midnight.

Milena felt his breath on her right ear. And then his lips buried themselves in her neck. He hugged her tightly from behind. Millions of goose bumps ran through her body again. Unable to control herself, she turned to face him, her arms wrapped around his head. Their lips met in a deep, passionate, long kiss. He took her buttocks in his strong hands and pulled her close to him.

– Stop, please, – she said, catching her breath.

– I can't. – he said, panting. – As soon as you're near me, I lose control. I become a boy who has to taste the fruit of love for the first time. I become weak. And the only one who can help me is you.

His words made Milena's whole– body tremble. Each of his words was a pleasant, warm stream flowing down her body. The trembling did not let her go, but on the contrary, thickened. Her heart was beating fast. She took his face in her palms again and touched his lips.

– I love you, Gor. – Milena said, looking into his black eyes. The passion– filled look made them both trembles again. He hugged her tightly. She nuzzled her face into his neck, breathing deeply of his scent and the warmth of his beloved body.

It wasn't until dawn that Gor left her, leaving behind pleasant memories. Despite his strong desire, he never touched his beloved body.

– Milena, did you know that a white– toothed smile is not the standard of beauty and health everywhere. Here, look," Ani said, running her thumb over her smartphone, "I'm reading an article: It is still very fashionable for Vietnamese women to cover their teeth black. Teeth used to be blackened not only in Vietnam, but also in Japan, Indochina and Russia. Black– toothed beauties could be found in Belozersk and Toropets until the 19th century. They did not have black varnish like Japanese and Vietnamese women, so they achieved blackness with the help of acids and also by rubbing their teeth with a mixture of titanium and acetic acid iron. It was thought to be good for health, but above all it showed that a woman belonged to the nobility. It also meant she was married. Can you imagine? It's idiotic. People have invented so many ways to whiten teeth, and these primitive women cover them with black varnish.

Milena had entered a new, unexplored stage in her relationship. It was frightening and attractive at the same time.

They walked, holding hands. From time to time he gently put his arm around her waist, kissing her cheek with even greater tenderness. Milena couldn't hide her genuine happiness and the smile that never left her delicate face. Her eyes burned, her heart leapt, her body was enveloped in a special warmth, her soul rejoiced. In spite of the people passing by, Milena also did not miss a chance to kiss her beloved. Judgmental looks could not be avoided. The mentality of the people was slowly changing.

But they didn't notice anyone around them. For them, the streets, parks, squares, houses and cars were empty. For them there was only Him and Her. The sweetest feeling in the world. When of all the various emotions and feelings in the body rages only love. It's moments like that that are worth living for. These are the moments when life is perfect. It's moments that are remembered forever.

– It is getting colder. What do you think?

Gor and Milena sat in the hospital garden. She laid her head on his shoulder and watched the yellow leaves fall. Winter was just around the corner.

– I agree. – Milena said without raising her head. – Where shall we go? To Aragats? Or is it impossible to get there?

– No, why not? I'll call the guys," Gor said, taking his phone from his pocket.

While Gor made arrangements with his friends, Milena watched with special interest as the withered, curled leaves fell one by one, covering the lawn.

Every autumn, Armenians "open" the season of khash (rich broth made from pigs' feet), one of the oldest Armenian dishes. The word "khash" comes from the Armenian word "khashel", which means "to boil". Khash was the food of the poor as it was made from leftover meat and often bones.

Milena, Gor and Ani and the rest of their friends went to Aragats to taste the national dish. Aragats is an isolated mountain range in western Armenia. It has four peaks. On one of the slopes of the mountain system, at a high altitude, is Lake Kari, which is reached by a narrow, long, winding road covered with snow from September to early May. It can be very difficult to get there, but that doesn't stop interested visitors and khash lovers. There is a large restaurant on the shore of the lake where the young men used to go.

Having eaten enough khash and drunk enough vodka, the young men sat comfortably on large wooden chairs around a huge table in a separate room of the restaurant designed for a certain number of people, talking, telling jokes and reminiscing about their student days.

– If your husband is not rude, does not drink, does not annoy, does not sit in front of the computer, does not go to the sauna with his friends, does not watch football, poke him with a stick – it looks like he is dead.

Mukuch's anecdote brought a roar of laughter.

– Don't start, Mukuch, said Anna, his wife, laughing.

– Why? Isn't it? – said Mukuch, looking at his wife. – Would you like to have such a dead man around you?

– Of course not! – exclaimed Anna, hugging and kissing her husband.

Mukuch kissed his wife in return. Milena, smiling sweetly, looked at the newlyweds, sat down next to Gor and laid her head on his shoulder.

– Wife to husband on the phone: My computer doesn't work. Did you press the big button? Yes, I did. Did you plug the cord into the socket? I'll take a torch and look. What's the torch for? There's no power.

Loud laughter filled the room again.

Have you heard that? – Gor asked, throwing his right arm

over Milena's chair, fingertips touching her shoulder. – A hospital room. A knock at the door. A nurse enters, walks over to the patient and abruptly rips off the blanket. Then she takes a razor and shaves the patient's pubic hair, then turns him over and shaves his arse. He gives an enema, inserts a candle and turns the patient onto his back. The patient looks stunned: Can I ask you a question? Tell me, why did you knock on the door?

Weekly meetings with friends, daily dates with Gor, every minute communication with him. Milena's days were filled with all kinds of positive emotions. Her phone was full of their shared photos and silly videos, meaningless but most important corre-spondences. Milena loved revisiting and re– reading them. At the same time, the smile never left her face.

"You know, Astine, I think Gor will introduce me to his par-ents by New Year's Eve. He's already dropped a few hints. It's the most exciting and long– awaited moment. You have no idea what I feel when I imagine it. I'm waiting for this day with bated breath.

I think if everything goes well, and I hope it does, we can get engaged in February. And in the summer, when Aren comes back, we'll be married.

Don't you dare laugh, Astine. I know you're reading this and smiling at the stupidity and naivety of a grown– up girl. But don't judge me, please. Love made me this way. But I'm glad. I'm glad, Astine.

If I'd known it would be so wonderful, back at the cottage, I wouldn't have done that to Gor. I regret every minute I lost, every minute he wasn't there.

But things will change. It already has.

Thank God.

Don't forget to give my regards to Armen and kiss him for me."

Chapter 5

December, 2015

"My dear Astine. Not a minute went by that I didn't think of him. My breathing stopped as soon as I saw the scenes of our first and last night together. His kisses – deep, tender, passionate. His hands – constantly caressing my body.

The pain he caused me was terrible and unbearable. But the happiness he gave me was the greatest and incomparable.

Interesting. An ordinary day, ordinary feelings, or say, the worst day of the calendar, when it seems that there is no way out, that everything is going down the drain, that life is going to hell, that you are the worst person on Earth, that you have the worst, most meaningless and thankless job, that everything is just worse than ever – one call, one call from the right person can change everything. All problems will be solved, work and life will make sense, you will become the happiest and most successful person on the planet.

He didn't come again. She watched the clock, counting the minutes and holding her breath, hoping the phone would ring, that she would hear his passionate, longing voice. But it was all a pipe dream. She never saw the long– awaited name on the screen of her smartphone.

For more than a week, Milena could not meet Gor. He answered the phone, but then quickly disconnected under some pretext. Milena thought Gor had some problems at work, but deep down she felt something was wrong.

He finally replied to her numerous text messages and arranged a meeting which he never showed up for.

Milena could barely keep herself from going to his office. He didn't show up at the canteen. Milena had lunch with her friends. She often saw Gor's colleagues at neighbouring tables. She did not dare to ask or find out anything.

She had her smartphone in her hands day and night. She spent days going over all the possible and impossible mistakes she could have made that would cause Gor to behave this way. But nothing came to mind.

– Can we talk today?

– About what?

– About us.

– I don't know. I've got things to do. If I get some time, we'll talk.

– Can you try to free it up? – Yes. It's very important.

– I'll try.

After another short dialogue with Gor, Milena switched off the phone and put it down on the table, laid her head on the pillow covering her eyes. Her heart clenched in her chest. The unpleasantly nauseating tugging inside wouldn't let go. Unable to hold back any longer, Milena got out of bed and walked briskly across her small room. Back and forth, back and forth.

She wasn't thinking about anything. The lump in her throat was choking her. The pressure in her chest increased. Milena suddenly covered her mouth with her right hand as another wave of nausea hit her.

She couldn't eat or sleep. Milena woke up in the middle of the night, looking hopefully at her smartphone. There were lots of notifications, messages from her friends. But it was silent.

– What's wrong with you, Gor? What's wrong? I can't take it anymore. It's winter outside, but I'm suffocating. The house is warm, but I can't stop shivering.

– So? What did you want to talk to me about?

She didn't know where to start. He'd never been this rude to her before. She had rehearsed their entire conversation before meeting him. But when it came time to speak, she was stunned, hesitant to say a word. They hadn't seen each other for ten days. His call had surprised her, making her shiver, smile, feel sad, her heart race.

But when he saw him, he was confused. Something about him had changed: his look, his speech, his movements. Somehow, he was strange, frightened, out of his depth.

"What's the matter with you, Gor? You're scaring me. What's the matter?"

– And? What's the matter? Say something. Have I cancelled all my business just to hear your silence?

She only shook her head. A gentle hand passed over his unshaven cheek. Tears covered his eyes. Filled to the brim, they trickled down her cheek.

– Milena, what's wrong? Come here.

He hugged her gently. Suddenly Milena felt a small spark of hope. In this cold stranger she felt a piece of her Gor.

Milena struggled to rest her head on his shoulder. Tears were choking her. Her heart was breaking. He had never held her so tenderly before. She felt happy and loved again.

– Please don't let me go. – Milena could only say through her tears.

– Why do you think I'll let you go? – Gor said, squeezing her even tighter into his arms.

– I don't know. – she said, cuddling into his chest.

– Look at me. – Gor said, releasing her from his embrace.

Milena couldn't lift her head. Gor took her by the chin and gently lifted her head himself. Milena looked up at him with tear–red eyes.

– It's all right, do you hear? I'm sorry for my harshness. I didn't mean to hurt you. It's just that I have some problems that I don't want to burden you with. That's why I've been avoiding seeing you lately.

– But, Gor, I'm always here for you. For better or for worse. If you have a problem, share it with me, talk to me. Even if I can't help you, at least you'll talk to me. I really want you to be honest with me.

Gor abruptly got up from his seat. Headed towards the wall, on which there was a painting of a ballerina. Milena straightened up, sitting on the edge of the sofa and, with eyes full of tears, looked after Gor. Milena asked Gor to meet her in a private place to talk quietly. He picked her up at the clinic and they went to a café on Pushkin Street that had separate VIP rooms.

– I know, Milena," Gor began, still pretending to scrutinise the painting. – You are one of the only people around me who is always there for me. You are very dear to me.

He turned to face her, but he was looking nowhere. With slow, heavy steps he walked towards her, sat down beside her and hugged her again.

– Don't take offence, Milena. I would never intentionally hurt you. It's just...

– Gor. – said Milena, clinging tighter to her lover. – I know you care for me. I feel it. But I can't bear your indifference. In all those days that we haven't seen each other, I felt bad. I thought I'd lost you. Just the thought of it made me shiver. I was getting weaker day by day....

Gor pulled Milena against him with his right hand, kissing her temple and not letting her finish the thought. With each embrace, the hardened cold cells were filled with life and energy. Milena could feel his body and soul recovering from the freezing. Pressed against his chest, Milena inhaled the scent of his favourite body. Her heartbeat normalised, the constricted vessels dilated, a pleasant flow of warmth spread through her body.

The New Year was just days away. Despite the fact that many people had already bought and decorated their Christmas trees, there was no shortage of customers in the shops. Toys, jewellery, decorative napkins, themed tablecloths and many other items were in high demand.

The whole city was actively preparing for the New Year. Perhaps this is the reason why people, despite their financial situation, set the table properly and decorate their homes.

For Milena, the coming year was going to be special. Therefore, the preparations were also special. One of the most important events in her life was planned for this holiday – meeting Gor's parents.

But Milena was uneasy about Gor's minimal involvement in all of this. She spoke enthusiastically about their plans, but he just nodded his head. Milena thought his passivity was due to work–related problems. At least, she hoped it was.

But the unpleasant, strange feelings did not leave Milena. She put it down to the usual natural excitement before an important event. But...

– Ani, I'm confused, I don't know what to do.

Ani and Milena met after work in a café on Abovyan Street. The warm, cosy atmosphere of the beloved cafe and the fragrant hot tea with bergamot filling the airways were soothing and relaxing.

– What is it, Milena? – Ani asked, taking a small sip of the hot drink. – Things have been so confusing lately, there's no way we can talk. I feel something is happening to you. You're not yourself.

– Yes, Ani. Everything seems fine. But it's the worst. – said Milena, clutching a decorative cushion from the sofa. – Gor and I had planned to visit my parents for the holidays. There are only a few days left and he is still not talking. I wait every day for him to finally set a date and time, but ...

– Have you asked?

– More than once.

– And?

– He avoids answering directly each time. He says he's too busy. When the days get closer, he'll tell me.

– Well? There's still a couple of days left, right? Why are you so excited? If he says he'll do it, he'll do it. Don't worry so much, Milena. Everything will be fine.

The calm, gentle voice of the equally gentle Anja reassured Milena. But as soon as she thought of Gora, her friend's good charms dissipated. The tense shell was restraining her again.

– Ani, this isn't so much about me as it is about my parents. And I don't blame them. They're serious people who deserve to be taken seriously. Dad doesn't say a word, but I can see he's on edge too. Mum brings it up once in a while. But each time, hearing my silence and seeing my sadness, she doesn't want to bother me. And I don't want to talk to Gor about it anymore. I don't want to impose, you know?

– How is it going with him? Do you see him?

– Very rarely, Ani. He's either at work 24 hours a day or he's missing. Something's changed. Something's happened. And the worst thing is that he won't talk about it. I feel pathetic because I can't help him.

– Have you tried asking his friends?

– No, Ani. I don't want to, to be honest.

– What are you going to do then? – Ani asked, looking intently at her friend.

Milena lowered her eyes. She put the pillow down next to her and took a cup of tea with both hands, which had time to cool down. She took a sip. She lifted her eyes to meet Ani's.

– Waiting. – She just answered.

1st January 2016

"Hello my dear and beloved. Happy New Year. You have no idea how happy I am for you and Armen. I love you so much. It was the best start of the year. I'm going to be an aunt soon. Yay."

2nd January 2016

"If this continues for a while, I'm going to lose my mind. Either I'm over– dramatizing everything or everything really sucks. I'm drunk, Astine. I'm sorry I'm writing this late, but the emotions, the negative emotions, are off the charts.

I'm home alone. I drained a bottle of semi– sweet wine.

I've been calling him for two hours. No answer.

He wished me a Happy New Year last night.

As soon as the screen of my smartphone lit up with his name at midnight, you have no idea how the world around me blossomed and made sense. One call from him and that was it! What the hell, Astine?!

He didn't say a word about meeting me. Which is just not going to happen!

I'm so angry with him! So hurt, so depressed!

And after only a few drinks, I started calling him! A man, Astine, who just didn't keep his promises. He didn't deserve me. He had no right to do this. He had no right to do this to my parents. I hate him!

He ruined my party. He ruined my dreams. All the things I had planned for these days.

What if there was someone else in his life? What if he fell in love with someone else?

What the hell!

I'm so sorry. Please forgive me. Yesterday you gave me great news. And today I'm burdening you with my failed life.

I'm sorry again.

I just needed to talk.

5th January 2016

"Gor and I visited Mukuch and Anna today. He called yesterday, set up a time. I was going to not answer his call at all. And that would have been the right decision, given his behaviour. But I couldn't.

Everyone was there. It was great. Honestly, I wanted to talk to him afterwards, but I didn't. The day was so good, so positive, and he was so normal, gentle and kind that I just forgot everything that had happened. The whole monologue that I had been practising and rehearsing all these days was gone with just one passionate touch from him.

Chapter 6

January 2016

"I'm sorry for the overly explicit lines. But I can't be silent.

I closed the doors of my heart, but they opened so inappropriately. His mere presence, a glance, a touch was enough to throw away the keys of a broken lock.

Soft, slow kisses. His lips, his hands. I felt every part, every cell of his flesh. One kiss was followed by a million uncontrollable kisses. The passion grew with each passing second. My lower abdomen burned. Hands gripping his hair. Hands running down my back. He always lifted my blouse, exposing my stomach and back, stroking them. And they were eagerly covered with millions of goose bumps and warmth.

One day I went for a walk in the fresh air. It was a cold but sunny winter day. There was a light breeze. I put my hands in the pockets of my coat and walked slowly along Northern Avenue. Passers– by walked towards me. I looked at them and continued on my way. Suddenly a young couple caught my attention. Why it was her, you will understand now.

The girl was small, unattractive and unremarkable. But she immediately piqued my curiosity. The guy next to her was hugging her tightly. At first glance, it looked like an ordinary couple in love. But the girl's gaze did not escape me. Her eyes were on fire. I had never seen such sincerely sparkling, happy eyes.

That day I had another argument with Gor. I was wearing sunglasses. Tears were streaming from my eyes.

When a couple passed me, I stopped for a moment. How stupid girls are. What little things we pay attention to, missing the most important thing. I'm a tall, beautiful, successful young person with tear– stained, faded eyes and a broken heart. Why do I need my looks? Why do I need a golden shell if the inside is empty? If everything inside is ruined?

And her... Her eyes.

It's true, Astine. Nothing matters, everything is relative. The only thing that matters in the end is whether you're a happy person or not."

Milena often avoided her parents. She didn't want them to see her in that state. Often tearful and droopy eyes, a dull face. Her parents came home late. Milena would quickly set the table and lock herself in her room, pretending to be tired.

But she couldn't hide all the time. Milena's father decided to talk to his daughter anyway. Her parents understood her state of mind and did not want to interfere, giving Milena time to calm down and come to her senses.

– Milena, look at me. You deserve the best; do you hear me? I won't give you to anyone who makes you shed a single tear. I can't see you like this. I won't let you. Look at yourself in the mirror. What do you see?

Milena looked. A weeping face, frizzy hair falling over her eyes, a slouching body, her father hugging her tightly from behind.

– Look closely, Milena. Do you know who you are?

Milena shook her head negatively.

– If you knew, if you valued yourself as much as everyone

around you does, you wouldn't be standing here like this. Daughter," he turned her around and looked into her tear– red eyes, he doesn't deserve you. Please let him go. If you don't, I will kill him with my own hands. Then he will be out of your life forever.

Milena couldn't say a word. Tears streamed from her eyes. Her heart clenched and hurt. It hurt a lot. No one understood her. No one accepted her feelings. She knew, she was sure, that her father's words were true, but she couldn't help herself.

She hugged her father tightly.

– I'm sorry, please. I didn't mean for this to happen.

– Don't apologise to me, Milena. – Don't apologise. It's not your fault.

Her father squeezed Milena even tighter in his arms. Milena felt an inexplicable strength flowing through her veins.

"I should be strong. I shouldn't have to bend over like this. For them. For those who really love me. For those who will always be there for me, no matter what the circumstances.

After talking to her father, Milena thought for a long time. She weighed the pros and cons. Then she decided to take radical steps, then she stopped. More than once she wrote a firm letter with exclamation marks, which she never dared to send. She deleted it with a flick of her finger. At that moment she sighed freely. But was that what she really wanted?

"I didn't know what decision to make, Astine. I didn't know what was right. For my desires were far from the truth, from the reality around me. I had two choices: to leave things as they were, closing my eyes to what was happening, or to put an end to it all, to extinguish myself day by day without it. In both cases I came out of the game defeated. It wasn't my game. It wasn't my victory. And that was the one undeniable truth.

He came up behind her and hugged her tightly. She didn't react, but her body was shaking and trembling. He turned her to face him, looked at the door, then at her lips. He tried to kiss her. She turned her head to the side, he touched his lips to her cheek.

– What's wrong with you?

– And you ask me that?

– I don't understand.

– Really?

– Yes.

– You're a real piece of work. Either you've got a bad memory or you're a great actor.

Milena pulled away, walked to the window and crossed her arms over her chest. She looked nowhere, just to avoid meeting his gaze. After all, just a glimpse of his eyes would be enough for her to soften and find herself in his arms again.

– Would you look at me?

Milena shook her head negatively.

– Your instability drives me crazy. – Gor spoke sharply but calmly. – I left my patients and came down to see you. And instead of a warm greeting, I get this? – He said, stretching his arms out in front of him.

Gor was wearing a blue medical uniform, over which was worn a knee– length white dressing gown with the buttons undone. On the left pocket of the gown was a badge that bore Gor's piercing gaze. A black cap with a picture of the particles of the universe protruded from the right pocket at the knee of his trousers.

One of the distinguishing features of surgeons is their caps. Many doctors collect a whole collection of all kinds of colours and with a variety of images. This small accessory makes the image of the doctor interesting, special and sometimes funny, and is also a fruitful means against phobias of patients. Recently, multi– coloured gloves and masks have also become fashionable. Every doctor can add these little nuances to his image and emphasise his individuality.

– I want to talk. – Milena said suddenly, turning to face Gor but still avoiding his gaze. Milena sat down at her desk, leaning back and covering her face with two palms. – I can't be silent any longer.

– About what? Speak, I'm listening. Do me a favour, put your hands down and look at me.

Milena dropped her hands obediently. But she didn't look up right away.

She got up from her seat and approached Gor. Finally raising her eyes, she met his black ones. Her heart pounded. The ring finger of her left hand went numb. Milena wrapped her fragile arms around Gor's neck. The scent of his perfume immediately touched her respiratory receptors. Milena swallowed with difficulty.

– Gor, please, let's break up.

Her words were as unexpected as the gentle embrace.

Gor grabbed Milena's elbows and pulled her away from him, looking at her in surprise.

– What does that mean? – he asked, not letting go of her arms.

– I can't go on like this, do you understand? – said Milena, looking at him intently.

– Well, Milena? – Gor asked, squeezing her hands harder.

– Let me go. You're hurting me. – Milena said, pulling away, taking a step back.

– Answer me? I'm talking to you.

– Do you think what's going on is normal, Gor? – Milena's voice trembled. She couldn't believe she was finally saying out loud everything she'd wanted to say for so long. – We were getting engaged. What happened? You never said anything. You didn't even try to explain.

– Don't be dramatic, Milena. – Don't be dramatic. I told you I'm in trouble. Don't be so selfish.

– What? Me? Selfish? So, is it my fault too?

– Don't raise your voice. Keep your voice down. The walls are paper. And there are patients in the next room. There's no need for everyone to hear.

Milena closed her eyes and breathed deeply. She sat back down at her desk.

– You really don't find anything strange about this? You think everything is fine and I'm just being dramatic?

– First of all, don't you dare talk to me like that. Secondly, calm down and live for today. Stop dwelling on it.

– God. – Milena was the only thing she could say. – Gor.

He didn't let her continue. He walked over to her, pulling her by the arm and bringing her close to him. Gor hugged Milena tightly kissing the top of her head.

– I just wanted to spend a few minutes with you. – He said in a calm and gentle voice. No need to spoil these precious minutes, Milena.

Milena was confused. She was ready to talk, to discuss everything, to sort things out. But...

– I wanted to...

– Later. Later you'll say everything. – Gor said with a special passion in his voice, taking her by the chin and bringing Milena's delicate face close to his.

With every micrometre getting closer to Gor's lips, Milena was filled with warmth. Her lips trembled in anticipation. Her heart froze, hesitating to beat and break the privacy of the lovers. Gor's hand moved gently down Milena's back. When he reached her waist, he pulled her close and kissed her passionately on the lips, while Milena's fingers sank into Gor's smooth black hair.

"End it all? End it? How, Astine? How can I decide to take that step when this man is changing my world with his mere presence?

You judge me, don't you? You smile when you read my letters. I know you are. I complain. Then he appears and I'm happy again. Then he's gone again. And so it goes, day after day. Week after week. I'm caught in a wheel from which there is no escape. One curve is heaven with him, the other is hell without him. And so it goes round and round. It's always the same.

And as long as this wheel keeps turning, there's no escape for me, Astine. But believe me, this wheel is the best and the worst thing that could happen to me"

Chapter 7

February, 2016

"I want to tell you something. I don't know why, but this snippet from my childhood I can't forget in any way. I was about eight years old. I was a very cranky kid back then. My parents poked and prodded me, trying to satisfy my every whim. One day, my mum and I were shopping for children's clothes. We wanted to buy me a pair of shorts and a T– shirt. I liked one set, she liked the other. We had different tastes at the time. She urged me to get the one she liked. I was adamant. I insisted. We bought the one I liked. But I never told her that the blouse was extremely uncomfortable and pinched my armpits. In silence, I put on my "favourite" set, feeling insurmountable discomfort. And every time I put it on, I felt very sorry for my folly. For not heeding my mother's words. And I still do. But as it turns out, I haven't changed over the years. And back then it was just a blouse... .

I was bored. I was trying to stop something that wasn't stopping. I was trying to kick out of my life the one person who could have been the source of my continued happiness.

The road back seemed so thorny, so insurmountable, that even looking back made me wince and look only forward.

And what lay ahead? A smooth path or thorns worse than the ones before? Where to turn? Where to go? I was lost. I stood still and waited. But waiting for what? What was I waiting for?

Sometimes I wished I could just close myself in a corner, turn off the light, lie down, close my eyes and be alone with him again. At least in my mind, but with him.

Time seemed to stop. His heart was beating wildly, unperturbed by the darkness and the lingering silence. Everything around him froze. And inside, a hurricane was raging. My ears buzzed. There was not enough air. The tiny cells around her stopped, afraid to anger the raging cells of her soul.

She took a deep breath, setting the air molecules in motion. Somehow her head became clearer. She opened her eyes, parted her lips slightly. Looked around. It was time. Her hands were trembling, goose bumps all over her body.

She opened the car door slowly, pausing for a moment.

Shouldn't we?

She did.

She stepped out of the car, closing the door with particular ease. Every muscle in her flesh was tense. It had taken her a lot of effort to get up to the third floor of his apartment, and even harder to find the courage to ring the doorbell.

– I missed you.

Silence.

– Why don't you say anything? – he asked, hugging her gently.

– I just have too much to tell you. – She replied.

– Then tell me. But before I start, I want to hear you say that you missed me too. – He said, looking into her eyes with childlike excitement.

Silence.

– And?

Silence again.

She was sitting in his room on his big bed with her back to him, leaning on his lap, playing with her fingers in his hair. He, half lying behind her, was looking at her body with a greedy, passionate gaze.

She felt his hand slide down her back. The goose bumps returned. Her abdomen burned. His hand moved gently down her spine. Her breathing quickened.

– Don't. Stop it.

She stood up abruptly. His hand stayed in the air. She walked over to the mirror and leaned against the console in front of her. She looked at herself.

"What are you doing with your life? What is he doing to you? Get rid of him! He's ruining your life. He's ruining everything you've built up for so long. You're losing yourself with him, girl. Pull yourself together and do it! It's now or never.

Caught up in her own thoughts, she didn't even notice him coming towards her. He hugged her tightly from behind and sniffed at her hair. He removed a strand of her hair, exposing the right side of her face and neck. His lips touched her ear with extreme tenderness. She shivered, closed her eyes and opened her mouth. His lips moved down leisurely, caressing her neck. Their hands entwined. The mind blurred.

"He's beside me again, and I'm in his power again. I'll never be able to stop it. I'm too weak. He's too strong."

– Stop!

– Stop! – Suddenly she said sharply.

She pulled out of his embrace. She turned to face him. She looked into his black eyes. They burned with her gaze.

– How I want you. – He said passionately.

She stared at his lips as they spoke the words she wanted. She wanted to cry out in response, to give herself to him, to merge with him forever, to press her naked breasts against his naked chest, to feel warmth, protection, love. She wanted the highest feelings that she could only experience with him.

– No, stop it. Stop it. Nothing's gonna happen. This has to stop. It can't go on like this. It's not right. It can't go on.

– Why not? What's stopping us? I want you. You want me. I know you do. I can see it in your eyes. They burn. They burn me. I've never seen such hot eyes. What are you doing to me, Milena?

– Gor, what are you talking about? What are you talking about? What the hell is wrong with you? This is not how I imagined my first appearance in your parents' house. And I especially didn't expect you to behave like this.

– Milena, baby, we're adults. – Gor said, and walked right up to her again.

– Get away from me. – Milena said and pushed him away. – Yes, Gor. We really are adults.

Milena turned to the mirror and looked at Gor through the reflection.

– A few months ago, you swore eternal love to me. Two months ago, we decided to get engaged. To get married in the summer. We had plans together, Gor. As a couple, not as lovers. You never kept any of your promises. I was always there for you. Believe me, I would have stayed with you forever. But the man I see now is not my Gor. This man wants me physically. That's all there is to it. Am I right? Tell me, Gor. Am I right?

Milena looked at him intently with pleading, frightened eyes. Her lower lip trembled.

– No. – You're wrong. – He just said, moving away from the

mirror and sitting on the edge of the bed.

– Then why don't you introduce me to your parents? – Milena said, still looking at him.

– They're not home today. – Gor replied, lowering his eyes.

– I'll come tomorrow.

– Milena, don't start again. I told you, when the time comes, everything will work itself out.

– When the time comes? Are you kidding me? Are you? – Milena looked at Gor sharply. She had the feeling that she was slowly losing control of herself.

– Don't you dare talk to me like that! – Gor said, also raising his voice.

– My God, Gor. You've never raised your voice to me before. You've never been so hard on me. I just can't believe it...

– You're forcing me, Milena. – You're forcing me. Behave properly and you'll get a proper answer.

Milena froze for a moment and covered her eyes. She went over to the bed and sat down next to Gor. And with a calm voice she continued.

– Why did you come into my life? What do you want, Gor? Let me go. And if you can't, then let me into yours. Stop toying with me, with my feelings. I hate myself for how much I love you. This feeling, I don't even know what to call it, I forget everything. I am losing myself. I'm losing my self- esteem. And that makes me hate myself even more. Oh, God.

– Shut up, you hear me? You shut up! Shut up! Will you shut up? Don't say another word. – Suddenly Gor said, standing up abruptly. He went to the window

– Make me shut up! If you say anything to make me shut up, I swear I won't say another word. I promise.

— What do you want? What do you want to hear? — he said, turning to face her.

— I want to hear many things from you. I want things you can't give me. You don't want to be with me, you don't want to tie your future to me. But you won't let me go! What do you want? Tell me. What do you want?

— I just want to be with you.

— I've heard it a hundred times. — I've heard it a hundred times. I'm tired of it. What you want and what you do doesn't make any sense.

— Shut up. Stop talking rubbish.

— It's not bullshit. It's the brutal truth. The only time you think about me is when you've got nothing else to do and you're completely free. The rest of the time you don't even think about me! Tell me, am I wrong?

— Is that what you think of yourself? Is that how you feel about our relationship?

— You make me think of myself that way. — You make me feel this way about myself. You make me feel this way.

— Come on. Shut up. I'm getting on your nerves.

— I'm always bothering you. I'm always wrong. I'm always wrong. Why did I even come here? It was a big mistake.

Milena left Gor's room and crossed the corridor to the front door. The door was locked. Milena tried to open it, but it wouldn't budge. Giving up her efforts, Milena paused for a moment and slid down the wall to sit on the cold floor. Her eyes filled with tears. And drop after drop began to trickle down her cheek.

After a few minutes, Gor stepped in front of her. He slowly walked over to her, sat down on the floor beside her and leaned against the wall.

– I'm sorry, Milena. – He began, looking at nothing in particular. – I know I've been very rude. I'm sorry for that. You drive me to it, there's no denying that. Especially when you know my character and my temperament.

Milena, leaning against the wall, listened to him in silence. Tears were drying on her delicate cheeks. Her eyes were red. She only blinked occasionally. Her breathing was barely audible.

– I have to be honest with you, Milena. – Gor said, looking at Milena. He took her cold right hand in the palm of his hand. Milena didn't react at all. – Everything is really messed up. But it's all my fault. I'm going through a difficult time in my life that I can't share with anyone. Not even you. I'm sorry.

Milena's eyes were fixed on the front wall, where she wanted to see something. But a new flood of tears blocked her eyes, clouding her vision. She listened intently to his every word. But try as she might, she expected and longed to hear something else.

– I don't know what to tell you. I don't know how to stay away from all this.

Gor turned his head again, letting go of Milena's hand and looking in front of him. He rose abruptly from the floor, turned to face the wall and pounded his fist hard. Milena still sat motionless.

– Say something. Don't just sit there like a dead person. Scream at least. Make a sound.

Milena slowly raised her painful eyes to him. She slowly rose from the floor as well, not letting go of his gaze.

– What do you want, Gor? – she asked in a quiet, calm voice. – What are you suggesting? I want to leave here with an answer, some kind of solution. I do not want to eat myself up day after day without finding an answer.

– I'm asking you to give me time, Milena. – Gor also said

calmly. – It's hard for me to analyse anything right now and give you an adequate answer.

– How much time do you need?

– I don't know. I have to sort out my feelings, Milena. And I really don't know when I'm going to get my head together.

Something in my chest tightened. The pain travelled down my left shoulder to my shoulder blade. Her legs weakened but remained stiff. All she could do was smile slightly.

– Good. – Milena mumbled and grabbed the handle of the front door. But when she remembered that she couldn't handle it just a few minutes ago, she stepped away from it. – Open the door, please.

– Are you leaving already? – Gor asked, taking her hand.

– Yes. – It's late. – She said, pulling her hand away.

Gor, with one fleeting movement of his hand, handled the lock, opening the door. Milena, without a word, took a step towards the exit.

– Wait. – You're just gonna leave like that? Without saying goodbye?

Milena turned her head to Gor, smiled slightly again, stretched out, and with her tear– damp lips gently touched his left cheek. And, without another word, without turning back, she left the flat. A few seconds later she heard the sound of the door closing.

Chapter 8

March, 2016

"Spring". Just the word and the number on the calendar make you calm down, take a deep breath, fill yourself with hope that has had time to fade during the long winter nights. Too bad, Astine, that you didn't see it all. The spring of 2016 has begun magically in Armenia. Everything is as in the book. A blossoming city, singing of returning birds, sunshine, pleasant warmth, beautiful people who had time to change into spring dresses, shoes and cardigans. All– consuming love and good cheer. Even illnesses were somehow smoothed over and unresolved problems were solved.

Unfortunately, spring did not come for everyone. Despite the blossoming world around me, I only noticed its bare and prickly sides. Try as I might, I could not share the optimism of others.

The remnants of withered leaves swirled and fell onto her balcony. She leaned against the railing and watched for the slightest movement. It was only an hour before dawn. She couldn't sleep. It was chilly. You might even say cold. She breathed in the fresh air and waited for a change. But nothing happened. The inner pain continued to torment her. She smiled from time to time, tried to be happy about the spring, the new day, life, and to hide all the negative emotions, but nothing worked. There was a dead silence all around. The city had not had time to wake up, and she was glad about that.

She remembered his recent words: "I need to sort out my feelings. The latter chilled her body and heart more than the cold breeze of a March morning wind.

"I can't believe it. This just can't be happening."

Her heart still struggled, but her mind told her it was over.

"It's not over, is it? He won't let me go. I know he won't. I can feel it. But it's only passion that keeps him near me. "Nothing else. No real feelings. No love. I may not admit it to others, but there's no point in lying to myself.

And I do love him. And I'm so stupid. I want to close my eyes. I want to erase everything. Erase him from my memory and from my heart. If only it were as easy as erasing a line from a page of my endless letters.

If only I could rip out all my feelings and be as cold as this morning. But the sun will rise soon, the cold will be replaced by a pleasant warmth. Even cold doesn't last forever."

The leaves continued to fall. She looked at the only tree in front of her balcony. Autumn and winter had passed, and some leaves were still struggling to cling to the bare branches. They withered, curled, darkened, but they continued to fight for their place.

She smiled. She was like those leaves. She was holding on to something that had long since let go of her. She had changed in the past three months. She had gone from a fresh green leaf to a yellow lump. He'd drained her, taken all the life out of her. She was ready to bloom.

And yet she continued to cling to her withered branch. Even though her time was long gone.

"What shall I do? What shall I do? Should I hold on to the yellow leaf or should I let go and blossom again? What if it won't happen again? What if this is the only chance I'll get?"

– Milena, your phone is buzzing.

– Look at it, please. I can't answer it now.

– It's just the letter G and a planet symbol next to it. – Milena. Answer it?

Milena looked at the nurse confusedly with the tooth extractor in her hand.

– No. Leave it. – She said abruptly.

– Yes, of course. It's just that you told me to answer it.

– Yes, I know, I'm sorry for my abruptness.

– Nothing. – Alina replied gently and went over to the dentist's chair where Milena was removing a young woman's wisdom tooth.

– Well, that's that. Your tooth is out. – Milena said and showed the patient the extracted tooth.

– Why did you want to see me?

– I missed you.

Milena smiled.

– And what does that mean?

– Your lies are killing me.

Gor grabbed her face. Milena screamed in surprise. He clamped his mouth over hers. She pulled away.

– You're crazy. Let me go, you're hurting me. What are you doing?

– Don't call me a liar. – Don't you dare. I'll cut your tongue out.

– You're crazy.

She turned her face to the glass. She wanted to scream, to hit him, to get out of the car and slam the door behind her. But all these scenes were only in her head. She was too much in love to do any of that.

– Look at me.

– I don't want to.

Milena crossed her arms over her chest and continued to stare at nothing.

– Look at me. – He said again, but in a calm and quiet voice. She just shook her head.

He took her chin and turned her face to his. His black eyes devoured her. All the anger that had built up inside her against him slowly disappeared. She was filled with warmth and happiness again.

– Why are you doing this? I don't deserve this. Why are you hurting me, Gor?

Her voice was soft, gentle, with a slight tremor in it. Her eyes sparkled, despite her inner turmoil and sadness. He was there for her after all.

– I don't know, Milena, I swear I don't know. – Gor said, embracing Milena and holding her close to his chest.

And she, tucked into his T– shirt, drew from him everything she could dream of at that moment.

"How I want to merge with you forever. How I don't want to let you go. I don't want to forget, to kill all these feelings inside me. You're the only one with whom all this is possible. The only one who can bring me down to hell and lift me up to heaven."

He stroked her straight hair gently.

She lifted her head and looked into his eyes. She just silently admired him.

"I can't do it without you. I know that. But I can't stay with you either."

– Gor, can I ask you something?

Mm– hmm.

– Don't you love me anymore? – Milena continued without letting Gor answer. – Why did you say you had to sort out your feelings? You told me you loved me, and more than once. What's changed, Gor? Maybe it's my fault. Tell me.

– You said one question, but you asked several. – said Gor and continued to embrace Milena. – It's all right, my girl, it's all right. Everything will be alright. Everything will be fine again. It just takes time.

– Gor," Milena said, coming out of her lover's embrace and looking at him tenderly. – I'm willing to wait as long as it takes. I'm always here for you, do you hear me? I just need to know that you need me. And I'll never leave you.

– I need you, Milena, I need you very much. – He said after a moment's hesitation, looking intently and passionately into her eyes.

A soft meeting of lips, entwined hands, closed eyes, a fast heartbeat, passion and love.

Bands from all over Armenia and guests from abroad performed at Ulikhanyan's club every night. Many of them had already won the audience's sympathy, while others were just taking their first steps towards success. Every night the club was full. If you wanted to taste beer, wine or an original cocktail and listen to quality music, you had to book a table in advance.

Milena was a frequent visitor to the club of Vardan Ulikhanyan, an optimistic and cheerful young man, and his inimitable wife Arnella, who made this club one of the best places in the capital with their sincere care.

More than once Vardan offered Milena to perform on their small stage. Milena would have loved to have done so, but some strange circumstances prevented her and the young singer's performance was postponed.

It was on one of these evenings that Milena ran into her old friend, the most talented young composer, Aram Kirakosyan. Milena simply adored Aram's songs. They had a place of honour in her playlist.

– Well, my dear? When will you do me the honour of singing one of my songs?

Milena was sitting at a small table against the wall, slowly draining a glass of wine, when Arma, a short, black– haired man with a strange birthmark on his right cheek and sparkling black eyes, approached her.

– You won't believe this, but I was just about to talk to you about it. Vardan is free next Saturday. So, I thought, if you're free, we could have a concert.

– With great pleasure.

– I'm glad. – said Milena, taking a sip of semi– sweet wine. – Now we'll talk to Vardan, set the date and time, so he can do the publicity and the invitations.

Milena and Arma's concert was set for the 26th of March at seven in the evening. In just one week they had to choose songs, make some corrections and rehearse thoroughly because, despite their long friendship, it was the first time they would be performing together.

Milena invited her friends and friends of friends. Most of them promised to come. Despite their strained relationship, Milena also called Gor. He also promised to come, adding that he could not miss the chance to hear her voice.

Milena expected to see all the guests, but the most important to her was still Gor. It was his presence that she longed for most.

When he was in the audience, her voice sounded special. A note of excitement that gave every song an extra kick.

The long– awaited evening had arrived. It wasn't yet seven o'clock and the club was already packed. Only a few tables were empty. After Milena had greeted and seated her guests, she and Arma went backstage to prepare for the upcoming performance. Tight leather trousers, a smoky chiffon shirt with long asymmetrical sleeves, black high heels, a large ring with a black stone on the middle finger of her left hand and loose golden hair made Milena's appearance unique and spectacular.

Milena kept looking at the entrance and the clock. Her heart was racing. The excitement was indescribable. The ring finger of her left hand was numb again. Milena knew that as soon as she saw him, she would calm down and everything would fall into place. But he never appeared.

– Milena, I can't believe you're so worried. – Arma said, getting ready to go on stage. But when he noticed his friend trembling, he stopped and took her hand. – You have performed on big stages. More than once. And this is just a club where you know most of the people by sight. Pull yourself together and go on stage. It's ten past eight.

– Yes, Arma. – You're right. I don't know what's wrong with me.

Just then Vardan appeared backstage.

– What is it? Are you ready? – he asked, smiling his unique smile.

– Yes. – Arma said, looking at Milena.

– Yes, said Milena, smiling too.

– Then let's get started. – said Vardan and went on stage.

The young people came on stage after him and were greeted

with great applause. There was a piano on the stage and Arma sat down at it. Milena sat on a high chair in the middle of the stage, holding the microphone with her left hand and smiling at the audience. The fire in her eyes went out when she saw an empty table to the right of the stage. She lowered her eyes and took a deep breath.

As Arma began to play and the music gradually filled the room, Milena was enveloped in a kind of pleasant warmth, mixed with excitement and chills. Her body was covered with goose bumps and her heart was beating to the rhythm of the music. Closing her eyes, Milena brought the microphone to her lips and began to sing.

The songs changed one after the other. Each one ended with an ovation. Milena felt satisfaction, happiness. A hurricane of emotions raged inside her, the adrenaline level was through the roof.

Milena was looking forward to her favourite song from Arma, which she sang with special excitement and love.

After the concert and until late at night, Milena and Arma and their friends celebrated, drank and danced.

It was well past midnight when Milena hailed a taxi to go home. While waiting for the car, she looked at Gor's chat room, which had been online a few hours ago. Milena didn't want to find any more excuses for him. Not only had he not kept his promise, but he hadn't even written her a line.

"He was always there for me, Astine. He never missed a single performance of mine. Always supported me and was my most welcome audience. I guess his feelings must have really faded. Otherwise he wouldn't be acting like this.

It's heart breaking, Astine. But I must put an end to all this. For good this time.

I hope he doesn't call me again. I really hope so."

Milena had not found a place to be for a couple of days. Gor didn't call or write. She knew the best solution was to call it a day. But her inner ego wouldn't let go. Milena thought long and hard before writing. But considering the fact that when there is a yes or no, she always chooses the positive answer, Milena decided to send Gor a letter she didn't write overnight.

"I can't be silent anymore. I'm sick of being silent. Tired of eating myself up inside every time. Tired of looking at you and not saying anything. When there's a hurricane raging inside me. Don't you dare stop me. I've had enough. I'm going crazy. If I don't say anything tonight, I'll end up in a mental institution.

I love you. I don't just love you. I adore you. I love you. Crazy about you. You're on my mind 24 hours a day. Don't be surprised. Even in my sleep, I can't stop thinking about you. Wherever I am, my thoughts are with you. Your hands caressing my body, your lips kissing me passionately. Your body – when it presses against my flesh. The warmth that wraps around me when you press against me just a little bit. You are in me all the time. Even when you're far away.

It's not normal. I've become abnormal. I'm addicted to you. You're scarier than tobacco. I can't give you up. Quit. Send you to hell. Put a fucking stop to it. I can finally breathe. I don't want to breathe in a breath that's not even a little bit of you. I want to breathe you out completely. If I have to, I'm willing to cut my whole body to let you drip out of me. I'd do anything to make you go away. Gone forever. I don't want to know you. I want to erase my memory from the day I first saw you. The day you walked into my life at first sight.

You have no idea how I feel about you. I hate myself for it. Because I've never loved anyone more than me. And with you, I forgot myself. I forgot who I was. I've lost my value. And I deserve better. I know that.

With you, I can't say no. I can cancel everything just to be with you. I could forget everything just to be with you. And you can only fit me in on your own time. You know the difference? I was blind.

I waited every moment for your call. Your short text. Just a few words. You only thought of me when there was nothing to do. And don't you dare resist. That's true. But it wasn't always like that. Unfortunately, you've changed.

I waited for your rare but sweet words. And you've been stingy with even that. In the last few months, you've only complimented me once. I've received millions of them from the outside. But your one time was more precious to me than a thousand others.

I know your body in detail, in millimetres. I know all your moles. I've kissed them more than once. And when you were far away, I couldn't get them out of my head.

I know. I'm sick in the head. I've become so helpless, sentimental, weak, unappreciative and weak– willed since you came into my life. I don't know how I got to this point. I had no sooner settled down than one day I became nothing without you.

But despite all that, I will never love anyone more than I love myself. I won't allow myself to be treated like that. I've turned a blind eye, forgiven you everything, accepted you for who you are. But I won't let you trample on my self– esteem. It's more precious to me than anything else in the world. More than you.

Don't try to get me back. You don't care. That's why it won't hurt you at all. You'll soon forget me as soon as someone else comes into your life, just like me.

And as for me, don't even think about it. I'll get over it. I'll be fine. Time will heal everything. It's cured me more than once. Saved my life more than once. I trust it. It's almighty. Soon you will disappear from my life and become my next song. And every time I sing it, I'll go back to the past where I left you. I'll be filled with pain at first, then indifference. And when it's finished, I'll forget its content. You're already a note that becomes a written page every day. There's nothing left. Soon you will disappear. Forever."

Sent.

Chapter 9

April 2016

On the night of 2 April 2016, clashes began on the line of contact in Nagorno– Karabakh (also known as the "Four– Day War") between the armed forces of Armenia and the unrecognised Nagorno– Karabakh Republic (NKR) on the one side and Azerbaijan on the other. It lasted for three and a half days.

On 5 April, the parties declared a cessation of hostilities. A bilateral ceasefire agreement along the entire line of contact between the Karabakh and Azerbaijani armed forces was reached at 12 noon during a meeting of the Armenian and Azerbaijani Chiefs of General Staff in Moscow.

The 2– 5 April 2016 military operation was the largest military operation since the May 1994 ceasefire agreement.

"You know, Astine, I didn't think there would be a moment in the 21st century when guys would go to the battlefield with guns instead of clubs, and bottles of beer instead of guns.

It's strange. What a life. You don't know what the new day will bring. It doesn't matter what century, what year, what season, what country, what nationality. Nobody is immune to tomorrow.

Laughter, jokes, anecdotes, jokes can be replaced in an instant by a heavy silence. A stone in my soul. Tears frozen in my eyes. A lump in your throat.

A moment when you want nothing. Nothing at all. All feelings and emotions are dulled. There's nothing but emptiness in and around you.

You're sitting in your flat, where you've lived all your life. But you look around in a strange way. It seems to you that you are in a strange, unfamiliar place. You want to get up, open the door and run away... But where to? There's nowhere to go. Everything around you has changed. Everything around you is the same. Only you have changed.

"The Four– Day War" took with it more than could be imagined. Hundreds of young lives, hundreds of broken families, hundreds of extinguished hearths, hundreds of broken hearts, hundreds of devastated eyes.

Milena sat in the flat, wrapped in a plaid, not moving, not blinking, but only breathing occasionally. The emptiness that filled the young girl's inner world was alien, unfamiliar, agonising, indescribable. She could not utter anything, say anything, make any sound. Ani rang incessantly. Milena was unable to even take a smartphone in her hands.

In front of her eyes were two images: two favourite men. Men who each in their own way filled her life with all the most beautiful things. Aren. Gor.

With her brother, her parents had somehow managed to keep in touch. He was fine. He was far from the border at the time of the skirmish. But despite that, the war was still going on. And he was there.

Milena never got to say goodbye to Gor. She only saw from afar how a delegation of doctors in an ambulance left the hospital in the direction of Karabakh. Among them was Gor. She could not approach him. It cost her an inhuman effort to restrain herself, not to approach him, to hug him tightly. For she did not know if she would ever see him again.

Just at the moment when the car drove out of the hospital and disappeared from sight, an incomprehensible, strange, dragging emptiness formed inside Milena in a matter of seconds. Everything was empty. The world around her was empty.

She's at the clinic. They're at the border. Around her, spring in all its glory. All around them is ruin.

"You wouldn't believe it, but I was willing to give up everything – my present and my future – just to have them both back safe and sound. I was ready to give up my life if that was the price I had to pay for their continued well- being and happiness. What is it, Astine? Is it love? What do I call it? When you're willing to sacrifice yourself without a second thought?

I was willing to do all that. And yet I felt like an idiot, like there was nothing I could do to bring her back.

All I could do was pray. I could pray quietly in my room. So that my parents wouldn't accidentally hear my sobs. Because they were hurting too.

The whole country was on its feet, Ast. Fathers and grandfathers went to the border to see their sons and grandsons. We had young, inexperienced 18- year- olds defending us. And they really needed support. Every day we received news of heroically killed soldiers. And each time our hearts were torn apart.

Mothers, sisters, wives and grandmothers were only held back by their physical inability to help their boys. They could have fought the enemy with their bare hands. After all, the spirit of an Armenian woman is indomitable.

Clubs, pubs and other places of entertainment were closed. Young and old alike were silent. No one could work, eat or sleep. The country was covered with an impenetrable "polythene".

– I want to go to Karabakh.

– Are you crazy? No one will let you go. What will you do there?

– I will be next to them. I'll fight beside them.

Tears kept dripping from Milena's eyes. But her voice didn't break. She held on with all her strength.

– An, I can't sit here and do nothing anymore. I look at the kill list every day with bated breath. You have no idea what I go through each time. And every time I can't find their names, I thank the Almighty. I pray for them day and night. It's like a time bomb that could go off at any moment. If anything happens to them, I won't survive. It's not just words, Ani. I know you understand me. I know what's going on inside you every time you don't find Aren's name on the lists.

Ani looked up at Milena in astonishment. She smiled through her tears.

– I know. I've always known. But I never made my thoughts public. I hoped you would tell me when the time was right.

Ani threw herself on Milena's neck without saying a word. Finally, she gave vent to the tears that had tormented her for so long and said.

– I love him, Milena. I can't live without him. I couldn't bear to see his name on that damn list either. I have no one to talk to, no one to pour my heart out to, no one to cry my pain to. I've thought about going to see him more than once. About taking a gun and standing next to him, even though I've never seen a gun up close.

But I'd do anything to bring him back. Just so he'll live.

Milena took Ani's face in her hands and looked tenderly into her red, wet eyes.

– I'm sorry. Forgive me for being so lost in my own thoughts and suffering that I didn't notice your pain. Forgive me, my love.

– No, Milena. Don't. – Ani said through her tears. – It's my fault. I've always been silent. I was never honest enough with you. I was always the listener. I kept everything to myself because I was insecure. But I wasn't insecure about you, I was insecure about myself. I couldn't bring myself to trust you, to open up. I was always so closed. But things have changed. It's because of you. You opened me up. I started to feel, to live. To suffer and to rejoice. I discovered my feelings and I finally let them out. And as much as it hurt, I could finally breathe freely. With every word I uttered, I felt better, even though I actually felt pretty damn bad.

Days went by and still no news. She went to his page more than once, looking for some thread that would connect him to life. But the page was empty. Every time she saw that emptiness, an irresistible lump formed in her throat.

It was well past midnight. She lay with her eyes open. Dreams came one after the other, but her brain would not shut down. Her thoughts overshadowed her surroundings. She had forgotten she was in her room, in her bed. Thoughts surrounded her, took her out of reality. Time had stopped. Minutes flowed like a stream through impassable reeds.

"I can't forgive myself for not answering his phone call late at night. He texted me to pick up the phone, that he had something important to say. But I was so pissed off, so hurt about the concert, that I didn't think for a minute and just turned the phone off. The next day the war started.

Milena walked down Mashtots Street. Under the five– storey buildings there were branded shops. She glanced occasionally at the shop windows, but saw nothing. The mannequins in fancy dresses were naked plastic dolls with empty, meaningless faces. Expensive souvenir shops seemed to her like shops selling the usual junk. The flower and book shops that had always made her so happy were covered in a black and white film through which only a silhouette could be seen.

Everything was empty to her. The city was empty. The earth seemed to have stopped. The molecules stopped their disorderly movement. Everything around her froze. Nothing happened. Each day was the same as the day before. Time stretched like rubber. There was not enough air. She suffocated a lot.

"The war is over, Astine. It's finally over.

Strangely and eerily, Armenians have changed completely since the war. Our nation has been reunited over the past decades. Every-one, without exception, stood up for each other.

The war changed the personality of each person. People real-ised and began to appreciate the most precious thing in the whole world – life: sunrise and sunset, waking up after a deep sleep, touching cold parquet or soft carpet with bare feet, hot coffee in the morning, long– awaited dinner with the family after a hard day's work, and finally a peaceful sleep in one's own bed".

Aren was called a few days after the end of hostilities. He was fine. He just said a few words and promised to call as soon as everything was settled. Milena's parents realised that they could not expect any more information from their son over the phone.

Milena heard nothing from Gor for the whole of April. Her

heart was torn apart. Friends had kept her informed about his health. She knew that trauma surgeons were needed in Karabakh and that Gor might not return soon. It was this thought that comforted Milena every time she saw his page empty.

Chapter 10

May, 2016

"Distance. At school, this word was associated with the letter "S", with favourite algebra problems, with the formula "S=Vt".

And what is it now? I'm alone in my flat again. I am alone with my thoughts again. I'm alone with my thoughts again.

Distance. My parents come immediately to mind, my brother. My heart clenches strangely, my breathing is interrupted.

Distance. Now it's him and me. A bottle of red semi– sweet wine. A lonely glass in a lonely girl's hand.

Distance. Goosebumps. But it's not that. It's goose bumps of loneliness and longing.

I pick up my iPhone with my free left hand, swiping my thumb over the list of recent calls with a slight movement of my thumb.

Who do I want to call? There's no one I want to call. Almost no one. Again the memory sets its busy mechanism in motion. Again the shots of our love together succeed each other.

I put the iPhone next to me, waving my hand as if to dispel the visions. He's gone. Not in my life. The only thing between us now is distance.

The flight was delayed for five hours. Some kind of problem that nobody had announced. The only thing to do was to wait. Milena took a seat in the small waiting room at Zvartnots Airport, far away from the other passengers. She sat down in a comfortable chair, put a small bag beside her and stretched out her legs, put on her headphones and started scribbling notes in the notebook on her iPhone.

The idea of going to Moscow came about spontaneously. Her parents had immediately agreed that Milena should spend a few weeks with her aunt, an unmarried, middle– aged career woman who had moved to Moscow as a teenager and gone on to achieve great things. She had a big, cosy flat in the city centre, which Milena had admired more than once when talking to her aunt on Skype.

Milena didn't hesitate to pack her big crimson suitcase. She knew that if she thought about it for even a minute, she would change her mind. So, all the way to the airport, she distracted herself in every possible way. She even said goodbye to her parents in a hurry, trying not to notice her mother's tears.

Leaning back in her chair, Milena closed her eyes and turned up the music.

But even the loud music, the atmosphere and her inner struggle didn't help her to completely relax and stop thinking about him. Milena fought her inner "me and him" as hard as she could. At some point she succeeded. But as soon as she tried to relax, the thoughts of him would overshadow her inner world again.

– Excuse me? Excuse me?

Milena took her time to open her eyes and look at the source of the sound. A pair of blue eyes looked at her intently. She stood up and removed the earpiece.

– Sorry to wake you.

Milena hesitated before answering. She was fascinated by the handsome tall brunet who had so conveniently or not disturbed her privacy.

– Oh, no. I wasn't asleep.

– Yes. – You must have been. – The young man replied with a slight smile.

Milena looked at him questioningly, as if waiting for him to do something. The boy caught her eye and continued.

– Can I sit next to you? There are no seats left.

Milena was even more surprised because when she arrived, the waiting room was almost empty. But before she answered the young man, she looked around. And indeed, the room was full. Maybe she really had fallen asleep, because she hadn't noticed such a flood of passengers.

The guy continued to stand with a small sports bag in his right hand, a Rolex on his wrist, while Milena looked around in surprise. Suddenly, Milena quickly looked at her delicate gold hand watch.

– What flight are you on?

– Moscow. – Milena replied, while counting the time of departure.

– Don't worry, you're not late. There's still two hours to go.

– So, you're also...?

– Yes. – The guy answered, not letting Milena finish her thought. – So, can I sit next to you? I got up for coffee, and when I came back, some lady with a hat had taken my seat.

– Oh, sorry. Yeah, sure. Have a seat. Sorry again.

The guy sat down, putting his bag on the floor between his and Milena's chairs.

– No need to apologise. You were asleep. I'm the one who should apologise for waking you up.

– No, not at all. I should be grateful you woke me up, or I might have missed my flight.

– Yeah, that wouldn't have been good. – Yeah.

Milena giggled, imagining herself half asleep, having missed her flight. The guy laughed back.

– You have a great infectious laugh. – Yes?

– Yeah? – Thanks. A lot of people don't like it.

Milena, without realising why, lied. After all, almost everyone around her loved her loud, sincere laughter. Especially... Milena closed her eyes, trying to distract herself.

– Are you all right? You've become serious.

– Yes, I'm fine. It's just... Never mind. So, you're going to Moscow too?

– Yes. – The guy replied, stretching out his legs and crossing his arms over his chest. – I'm Vladimir, by the way. You can call me Vlad. – He said, extending his right arm.

– And I'm Milena. – Milena replied, extending her hand in return.

He shook it gently and released it just as gently. Milena would have been embarrassed before. Now she just smiled.

Milena made herself comfortable in the chair again, put her headphones back on, switched on Christina Si at full volume, quietly closed her eyes, knowing that as soon as the time came, her new acquaintance would wake her up. But rest was in no way part of the young man's plans.

– Milena? – Mi– le– na?

No matter how loud the music played, Milena couldn't help but hear Vlad's pleasant voice at her right ear. She reluctantly pulled out her headphones, pausing the song that had already taken hold of her.

– Yes?

– I'm sorry to interrupt again, but do you happen to have some kind of analgesic?

– Oh, I don't know. I'll look it up. – Milena said, starting to rummage through her bag. – In general, my bag is like a first aid kit, but I was packing so fast that I'm not sure if I took the pills. Why do you need them, by the way? Are you in pain? – Milena asked, pausing for a moment and looking at Vlad.

– Yes. – I have a toothache, to be honest. It started early in the morning, so I didn't have time to go to the dentist. I took a pill, it's better. But I don't think the analgesic effect has worn off. It hurts like hell. – said Vlad, rubbing his cheek and wrinkling his face.

– Here, I've found it! – Milena suddenly exclaimed, taking the pills out of her bag. – A toothache, you say? You're lucky.

– Why am I lucky? – Vlad was surprised.

– Because I'm a dentist. – said Milena, smiling. – But ironically, there's nothing I can do for you.

– Yes. – That's comforting. Now I feel even worse, realising that there's a cute dentist sitting next to me who won't be able to help me with my toothache.

– What do you mean I can't? – Milena was jokingly indignant. – I'm holding an analgesic.

– Yes, of course. Thank you. You're my saviour.

– Yes, I am. – Milena said, smiling wider.

Milena thought for a moment. What had become of that shy girl who would never talk to a strange guy. And now she was also flirtatious, despite the fact that she had chaos in her soul, which was what she was running from.

"Maybe my salvation has already begun?"

Two hours of waiting passed unnoticed. Fascinated by the conversation, Milena and Vlad were even surprised when the boarding for their flight was announced.

– Fora. – said Vlad.

– Yes. – Milena agreed.

And standing in the queue for boarding, their conversation did not stop. The seats on the plane were far apart. But it took Vlad a couple of minutes to transfer Milena's "neighbour", a pretty middle– aged woman who not only gave up her seat to a young guy, but also winked in support. The two and a half hours in the air also passed with heated conversations.

Vladimir turned out to be a very pleasant, modest, balanced, well– mannered guy. Thirty– three years old, his own business – a chain of restaurants all over Moscow, for the achievement of which Vlad worked tirelessly. After graduating from YSU, leaving his parents and younger brother behind, he moved to the big capital in search of prospects. For ten years of uninterrupted labour, he achieved a quiet and prosperous life, both for himself and his family, although the latter were no less well off than his hard– working son.

And so, several times a year Vlad travelled to Yerevan to visit his parents and his hometown, and then returned to the place where, as he said, all his dreams and goals had come true. Almost all of them.

– So, dear doctor, where can you fix my tooth? You won't be back to Yerevan soon, and you're not going to work in Moscow. Don't you feel sorry for me?

– Well, I suppose after ten years in Moscow, you've had a dentist. – Yes.

– First of all, yes. Secondly, having met you, I want to change my dentist. And thirdly, do you mind if we switch to "you"? Because "you" doesn't really fit in with our conversation.

– Of course, it's okay.

– Great. So, what are we going to do about my wisdom tooth, Milena?

– Extract it! – said Milena, laughing.

Hearing the beauty laugh again, Vlad's blue eyes sparkled.

She was sitting on the balcony, smoking her second cigarette. The smoke shimmered with raindrops. She watched it until it disappeared completely. And so with each exhalation of another puff.

"How nice it is here, away from you. How peaceful it is to breathe air that doesn't overflow with yours."

She did feel a calmness, a freedom away from him. She, closing her eyes, felt only one thing: peace.

"If I had known that just a week away from Yerevan and everything would fall into place, I would have done everything possible to make this moment come as soon as possible."

– If your parents found out I let you smoke, they'd send me to the afterlife.

Milena turned at the voice of her aunt, who stood in the doorway with her arms crossed over her chest, watching her closely.

– Be calm, All. They won't find out anything. – said Milena, continuing to watch the raindrops. – And anyway. I'm just messing around. You know that.

– Yes, I know, my dear. But that's how I started. Now I can't imagine my life without a cigarette.

Auntie took a couple of steps and found herself next to Milena. Leaning against the railing of the big balcony, which she simply adored, she gazed into the rain.

– It's nice. So peaceful. If it wasn't for you, I wouldn't have taken a holiday. I've forgotten what it's like to stay home and do nothing. I'm starting to like it.

– Really? – said Milena, smiling and putting out her cigarette.

– You and a housewife are two incompatibilities.

Alla looked at her niece resentfully.

– All, don't take offence. – said Milena, laughing. – You cook superbly, of course, but the role of a business lady suits you better than a woman in an apron at the cooker!

– Of course. – Alla said, sitting down next to Milena.

They sat in silence, looking at the raindrops, but seeing very different things.

– Don't you dare. – Alla said suddenly as Milena tried to light another cigarette. Suddenly she grabbed the cigarette from her niece's hand and put it back in the packet. – ☒? What are you trying to prove?

Milena continued to stare at the rain in silence. Her eyes started to get wet.

– Cigarettes won't solve anything. You've got to understand that. If you want to talk, I'm always at your disposal. Just don't take any more of this rubbish. – Alla said, throwing the cigarette packet into the corner of the balcony. She stood up and leaned against the balcony railing again and continued. – I know, I understand that you feel bad. Everything you've told me is really too much for a fragile girl like you. But that doesn't give you an excuse to get discouraged and hurt. I won't let that happen, ever. You're such a good girl, Milena. Very good. You're better than any of us, you know? And someone like you should be happy. But you've chosen a path that destroys you little by little with every step you take.

Alla turned to face Milena, leaning against the railing and crossing her arms over her chest. Milena, covering her face with her hands and sitting on her knees, said.

– Why are you starting this conversation again? Don't. I'm trying to forget him and you're bringing it up again.

– Now it's my fault too. – Yes. OK. I'm sorry. We won't talk about it again. Her mobile rings.

Milena lifted her head and looked at the screen of her smartphone, which was lying next to her on the small table.

– Aren't you going to answer? – Alla asked in surprise.

– No. Milena replied, resting her head on her knees again.

– Why? Who is it?

– Vlad.

– What is wrong with him? – Alla asked, but continued without waiting for an answer. – He seems a decent guy. Handsome, rich. Since the day of your arrival and day does not leave you without attention. And he's got a good idea about the clinic, good for him. I don't understand why you ignore him.

On the second day of Milena's stay in Moscow, Vlad rented a chair for an hour in one of the city's best clinics so that Milena could personally remove his wisdom tooth. She doubted until the last minute that she would be able to come to Moscow and completely forget about work. But the man's persistence overcame her principles.

– I can't, All. I just can't. – Milena suddenly said, lifting her head and looking at nothing. – At first I was fascinated by him. I even thought I was in love with him. Maybe I was. But... Something happened.

Alla looked cautiously at Milena.

– No, no! – Milena said sharply, noticing her aunt's startled look. – We just kissed. But, believe me, even that was enough to realise that I– . It's hard to explain. But he's not mine. Do you understand? – Milena looked at her aunt with a pleading look in her eyes. – He's perfect. I'm not going to lie. He's much, much better than Gor. But what I feel just by being with Gor is indescribable. It's happiness beyond description. It's boundless. All," Milena said, but suddenly hesitated, "I think... I think I'll never be able to forget him. I'll never be able to start a new life with another.

– Don't be silly, girl. I'm certainly not an optimist, but I can say with certainty that all this is only a temporary feeling. It passes. Everyone passes. Everyone gets used to living without each other. Although, to be honest, they never forget. Never– never. – Alla said with a special sad note.

Milena knew from her mother's stories that her aunt had a stormy affair when she was young, which her parents did not approve of. After the breakup, Alla went fully into work and achieved everything that people strive for throughout their lives. But the main thing in her life never happened. She remained alone: without a husband and children. According to her, she was happy with her loneliness, independence and carefree life. But all those who knew Alla well, felt that she was very happy to have a family and would have become an exemplary wife and mother. But the circumstances were not as Alla dreamed in her heart.

Milena, being a romantic person, hoped and believed that despite her stubborn character and age, her aunt would still meet her true love.

– I think you should give Vladimir a chance. He's a good guy, he's attentive. Talk to him. You've got nothing to lose. You don't leave for another fortnight. So you have plenty of time. – Alla said and went into the flat.

Milena sat there for a long time, looking at the endless rain that had been pouring since morning, as it seemed to her. But the rain stopped very suddenly. The sky began to clear.

– Milena, the table is set – Auntie's voice came out.

– I'm coming! – Milena shouted.

Within minutes the sky cleared. The sun took the wet city

in its warm embrace. It smelled of freshly cut grass, wet asphalt, evaporating moisture.

"Hello, my love. How are you? When are you coming? I miss you so much. I can't wait for Aren to come back. It's just days away. I can't wait to talk to you. I have so much to tell you.

Milena, there's something I need to tell you first. I don't know if I'm doing the right thing, but I can't keep quiet anymore.

I saw Gor a couple of days ago. He's back. A little thin, but mostly he was fine. He's fine. We said hello, said two words and then we went our separate ways.

Not a word about you. I swear.

I'm sorry I reminded you of him. But I know you were worried about him when you weren't even thinking about him.

He's okay now. I hope you are, too."

"Hello, my Ani. I can't wait to see you again. I have missed you a lot too. I have a plane ticket in five days. I'm coming back.

Thank God.

See you in Yerevan."

Chapter 11

June, 2016

"I'm writing to you hoping to hear something nice in return. I'm confused. Everything is all mixed up. But it's all my fault alone. "I met someone. I'm not going to give you a long description. I'll just say he's the best. That's all I'll say. You're probably wondering what the catch is. There isn't. I'm just confused.

He's perfect. But why am I not happy? Next to him, I keep looking at my mobile phone, hoping it will ring. With Gor, all I ever wanted was for time to stop and everything to stand still.

Sometimes I pick up a scalpel and look at it for a long time. I want to run the point all over his body, hoping to bring him out of himself. That's not normal. It's not love. It's a pathology. An incurable, slowly but productively killing disease.

It's only been a couple of days since I've been back.

Vlad promised to come back when he'd sorted out some things. As soon as he gets here, I'll introduce him to my parents. And I think we're going to consummate our relationship soon after that. He's very serious. Unlike Gor, he talks a lot about the future, about a future with me.

I've made up my mind, Ast. I've finally made a decision that has made me cry for many an evening. I know in time I'll get used to it. In time, I'll feel what I feel for Gor. And I'll forget the last one. At least I'll do my best to forget.

Yes. I will.

I heard a song in the waiting room at Domodedovo airport.

Sometimes I feel like they find me on their own at the right moment in my life. I have a concert in a month. I didn't know what to choose. And, strangely enough, this is the one I settled on. I fell in love with it from the first note. I hope you like it too."

The news of Milena's return spread with great speed. They met Gor in the hospital café. Sitting at a small table, Milena and Ani enjoyed their meal with great appetite. Milena was sitting with her back to the door, so she didn't notice Gor entering immediately. Ani's face changed dramatically as she looked towards the door. Milena immediately realised what had taken her friend by surprise.

There was no way she dared to turn round and look. After a couple of seconds, Gor walked by her side. He was with his friends. They sat down at a large table not far from the girls. Gor sat directly across from them. Milena couldn't look away for long. He stared at her intently. Finally she gave in.

Her heart hammered with all its might. Her left hand went weak. Milena put down her fork. With difficulty, she took a sip.

He continued to stare. She, even without looking in his direction, could feel his steady gaze. He only let go of her for a moment, and that was to light a cigarette.

– If you want, we can go out. – Ani said, noticing her friend's confusion.

– No. – It's okay. – Milena said with a tremor in her voice.

– Okay. Whatever you say.

Ani continued her lunch, and Milena couldn't touch hers anymore. The inner trembling would not let go.

– I'm sorry, Ani, but let's go out. – I can't stay here any longer.

I can't stay here any longer.

– Yes, of course. – Ani said, reluctantly left her unfinished lunch and followed her friend out of the cafe.

Milena hurried as fast as she could so she wouldn't accidentally look back. They quickly entered the doctor's room, which fortunately for the girls was empty. Milena sat down at the table. Ani stood next to her.

– Are you okay? – asked the equally excited Ani.

– No. – Milena replied sharply.

She leaned against the table and held her head with both hands. Ani looked worriedly at her friend, afraid to say anything.

– He did it again, Ani, he did it again. – Milena said, staring at one point.

– What, Milena? What has he done? – Ani asked, her voice trembling.

Milena lowered her hands, gave her friend a frightened look and whispered.

– He came into my life.

– Why are you avoiding me?

– I'm not avoiding you.

I've been calling you non– stop. And you never bothered to answer. What should I call him?

– I had a patient.

– For three hours?

– Endodontics on an upper molar. – You know how long that takes. You know how long that takes.

– I do. I do. I do. Okay. Let's say.

He took her left hand and pulled it roughly towards him. He wanted to kiss her. But Milena pulled away.

– What's wrong with you? – Gor asked, taking her hand again, this time without giving her a chance to escape. Milena gave in.

– Nothing. – She just said that, staring at nothing.

She was trembling. Her heart was beating out of her chest.

– Where did you get that drink? – You stink. You stink.

Milena stepped away from him, took a deep breath, looked intently into his black eyes and smiled strangely.

– What does that mean? – asked Gor, perplexed.

– Yes, I'm drunk. Too drunk.

– I realised that already. Why did you drink so much?

– I knew you'd do anything to see me tonight. That's why I drank all night, so I'd have the courage to be as honest as possible with you.

– We haven't seen each other for two months. I missed you. And to be honest, I was expecting the same from you. I hope you call this a revelation.

– Exactly, Gor. We haven't seen each other in two months and you haven't written or called.

– You know where I've been.

– I do, Gor. But that's just a meaningless excuse.

– Why didn't you call, why didn't you write? Weren't you worried about me?

Milena looked up at Gor and just smiled.

– I hate it when you smile instead of talking. – Gor said loudly and waved his hand.

– God, Gor. Enough! When did you get so picky and nervous?!

Gor said, as if he had not heard her last words.

– So? And what revelation were we talking about? Will you tell me now?

Milena shook her head negatively. The words were on the tip

of her tongue, but Milena controlled herself, hesitating to speak. But Gor, with his questions and his harsh tone, provoked her into an accumulated monologue.

– Come on, Milena. If you didn't miss me, if you didn't want to see me, then why are you here?

– How often do we part, Gor? – Milena began suddenly, standing close to Gor and looking him straight in the eye. – How often do we make dots that bring us together again and again? – After a moment's thought, Milena continued. – Have you noticed that the time between our quarrels and our reconciliations is getting longer and longer?

Gor looked questioningly into her eyes, which burned with a strange, frightening fire. She continued.

– The first time we parted, we couldn't bear to be without each other for twenty– four hours. The next day I was back in your arms. The second time we lasted a week. The third time, two. And this time we went two months without each other. I didn't hear from you for two whole months.

– What are you trying to say?

– That the next time might be the last. Unless, of course, it's already happened.

– Whatever it is, no matter how much time passes, when we meet we can't remain indifferent to each other. – Gor said, gently running his hand through Milena's silky hair.

– Gor, you can't imagine, but the last thing I want right now is to be here with you. But every time I'm near you, I forget that thought. And when I saw you today, two months later, I was convinced of it again. You possess me with just one look. You're everything to me. Even if you don't deserve it. I can't spend a minute without you. And I hate myself for it. I know we're nothing to each other, that we're only passionate, that we have no future. But in spite of all that, I'm here with you now. How I've changed. A year ago, I was the most ordinary, naive girl, who saw the world through rose– tinted glasses, whose life never contained anything reprehensible. And now...

– Do you regret us?

– I don't know. Hell, I really don't know. What have you done to me, Gor? What the hell did you give me? What do you want from me? What do you want?

– I want you to be happy.

– You want my happiness, but you do nothing about it. Why did you come back into my life if you're not going to see it through to the end? Don't you care?

– If I didn't care, I wouldn't have written and met you.

– Then how do you feel about me, Gor? Have you sorted out your feelings? Have you had enough time?

– Haven't you realised that I can't stand it when you talk to me like that? – You don't understand.

– Gor! Gor! Gor! I'm telling you how I feel and you're picking on my tone. Oh, my God! Hasn't anything changed in all this time?

– A lot has changed. You have no idea how much.

– How do you feel? Gor? Feelings?

Gor didn't say anything. He couldn't lie. In a short time Milena had learned a few peculiarities of his character. He could say something, evade an answer. But lie – never.

– Gor, you don't love me. – Milena said with a quiver in her voice, emphasising every word. – Please, let's break up. What do you need all this for?

Gor hesitated again. He lowered his head and thought about something. Milena had never seen him so confused.

– I won't let you go. – He whispered.

– What? Milena didn't hear him.

– I won't let you go. – Gor said louder, standing up abruptly. – You're not going anywhere from me. Never.

Milena was shocked. She couldn't believe what she was hearing. It was the first time in months that she had heard anything like this from him. But despite the kind words, Milena remained firm in her decision, which she did not like at all.

– You have no right. – she said suddenly, catching the confused look in his dark eyes. – I was yours. I was in your hands, in your power. I gave you everything. Everything a woman can give a man. – With each word, Milena's voice became more tender. There was a note of excitement mixed with insecurity, which was gradually dissolved by the alcohol playing in her blood. – I loved you. But you ignored my feelings. You neglected me. I shed so many tears for you, Gor. But I won't lie, I spent the best days of my life with you. But I don't want to be with you anymore. Let me go. Go away. That's enough. Don't make me feel this way. Because little by little I feel nothing. And that's the worst of it. I don't care anymore. I don't care anymore. And I don't want to. I don't want to forget and kill everything that happened between us. Don't kill yourself in me, Gor. Please. Leave some of it behind. I need it.

– I'm sorry, but I don't believe you. – I don't believe you. I don't think you really want to end it all.

– Yes. – I know. You have every right to think that. After all, we've had so many fights that I've never hesitated to get back together with you. But this time you'll have to believe me.

– Why all of a sudden? – Gor asked.

– I met someone. – said Milena, pleased with herself. Gor turned pale at her words.

– That can't be. – he said, trying to hide his true feelings behind a grin.

– You don't think I'm good enough to be liked by other people? – Don't be ridiculous.

– Don't be ridiculous. You love me. How can you do that...

Milena smiled.

– That's our problem, Gor. You're so sure of my feelings that you know I'll always be there for you, no matter what. But no. Just think, I could take a risk and try my luck with someone else. Yes, you're right. I don't love him. At least not yet. But he's so perfect, and his feelings are so real and genuine, that there's enough for both of us. And believe me, unlike you, he's not afraid to show them to me.

– Who is he? – Gor asked suddenly, after a moment's hesitation.

– You don't know him. We met in Moscow.

– So that's it.

– What?

– Nothing.

– And? You have nothing else to say to me?

– What do you want to hear? You've already said everything, the possible and the impossible. You've already made up your mind. All I have to do is wish you luck. – Gor spoke too calmly, too evenly, which left Milena perplexed.

– So that's it? – she asked anxiously. For the first time all evening she was afraid. The spell of alcohol was wearing off.

Gor said nothing. He quietly rose from his seat and walked to the door. He pulled the handle with his right hand, paused for a moment, turned to Milena, smiled strangely, bowed his head and disappeared behind the door without a word.

5 June 2016

"I expected a lot from our conversation, but not indifference. I thought that when I told him about Vlad, he would scream, hit me or go and look for Vlad himself. But the way he reacted really surprised and, to be honest, hurt me. I'd always thought, Astine, that a calm attitude was a sign of indifference. And that's what I feared most.

I'll try to remain calm. It was my decision. Gor wanted to stay, wouldn't let go. And I... The goddamn booze made me tongue-tied. But in the end, I said what I thought. I was honest. I was as honest as I could be.

I hope I don't regret my decision. I hope Vlad really doesn't disappoint me".

15 June 2016

"My friend Aren is back! At last my little brother is back. Dad and some of Aren's friends went to pick him up. There was a big surprise for him at home. We decorated the whole house with balloons, made a big poster with Ani: "Welcome home, soldier!", set the table, invited the closest relatives and all his friends.

When he stepped over the threshold of the house, a little gaunt, completely bald and pale, we could not hold back our tears. But they were tears of joy. The mother rushed to embrace and kiss her son. Everyone was crying. It was the most thrilling moment of my life.

When I hugged him, I felt complete and alive. My little brother, my twin, my blood.

At the table, my mother stood up and thanked God for bringing her son back safe and sound. Everyone stood up and drank with tears in their eyes to the health of all soldiers and to the repose of the souls of all fallen soldiers.

After the war, this toast became an integral part of every Armenian event.

Chapter 12

July, 2016

"What is it? An addiction or an obsession?

Who is it? God, the devil or a wanderer who just happened to show up in my life?

I knew this was the end. I had already reached the end of the line and no matter what, I had to get off, I had to continue my journey, but on a completely different route.

There may be only one in my life, but for me he will always be the first and the only one".

The idea of going to a nursing home came to Milena a long time ago, but circumstances did not allow it. Finally, when everything had stabilised to some extent, Milena decided to put her plan into action. After gathering all the necessary materials and consulting with her superiors and the management, Milena went to the nursing home with her brother, Ani and some other friends.

– We have a common room where all our residents gather during the day. It's like a children's playroom. – began the director after welcoming us cheerfully into his small office on the ground floor of the building. – Most of them are, and they are like children. We do our best to brighten their old age in some way, because the end is the same for all of us.

The visitors listened to the director in silence, occasionally nodding in agreement. He continued.

– You can go up to them. They're all there most of the time. The room is on the first floor. My assistant will show you there. Make yourself at home.

– Thank you very much. – said Milena.

The others just nodded and smiled.

They left the many bags of food and necessities they had brought with them in the warden's room. He thanked them and promised to make sure everything was distributed to the elderly residents today.

The boys followed a small, thin woman in her fifties. She walked slowly, so the boys had to slow down.

When they reached the first floor, the woman stopped at a white wooden door.

– You can come in. If you need me, I'll be in that room over there. – She said in a quiet voice, pointing to the opposite end of the long corridor, at the end of which she could see the same door.

– Good. Thank you. – Aren said, holding out his hand to open the door.

The woman smiled at the boys through her round optical glasses and was about to leave when Milena asked.

– Sorry. – The woman stopped and looked at Milena. She continued. – Are there any residents who are not in this room? Or is this where everyone gathers?

– To be honest," the woman replied after a moment's thought, "we do have one. She rarely leaves her room. Sometimes she even refuses to eat. But she's a very good and kind old woman.

– Can I go and see her? If it's possible, of course. – Milena asked.

Aren looked at Milena questioningly. Her sister's look was enough to stop Aren from asking too many questions.

– Yes, of course. – replied the woman. – Your room is one floor up. Come, I'll take you up.

Obviously discouraged, she reluctantly made her way to the stairs. Milena followed her.

She stopped on the first step and looked at her friends, who were still standing by the closed door, looking at her in surprise.

– You come in. I'll join you soon. – She said and went up quickly.

The room was small: grey, dusty walls, wooden but hard floors that were practically new. It felt as if it had rarely been walked on. The occupants of the room tended to occupy a small armchair by the window or a single bed in the corner.

– Come in, child.

– I'm sorry, I didn't mean to disturb you. – I thought you were asleep. I thought you were asleep.

– No, not at all. I've forgotten what real sleep is.

The old woman rose abruptly from the bed and looked carefully into Milena's eyes. The bed made a strange creaking noise and came to a halt. Milena froze in surprise.

– You come in. Don't stand in the doorway. – said the woman, waving her old hand.

Milena couldn't look away. The old woman's blue eyes fascinated her, but she couldn't understand why.

– Come in, don't be afraid of me. I'm just an ordinary old woman.

– I'm not afraid of you. – Milena said, a little embarrassed.

– Are you sure? – asked the woman with a special tone in her voice.

She lay down in bed again, this time quietly, without any sudden movements, looking up at the ceiling, crossing her arms over her chest and breathing only occasionally.

Milena watched her every move carefully. There was something strange, incomprehensible, unfinished about this woman.

– People are not afraid of me, no. I'm not that scary. – She said, smiling slightly, and continued, still looking up at the ceiling. – They are afraid of my image, of who I am. I am a prime example of loneliness. Loneliness in life and worst of all in death.

Milena felt her body covered with millions of goose bumps. Her eyes filled with tears and her heart clenched strangely in her chest. The woman didn't know anything about Milena, but she spoke as if she were talking to a kindred spirit. The thought made her heart squeeze even tighter.

– I wasn't always lonely, I wasn't always what I am now – just another old lady in a nursing home. – The woman went on, ignoring Milena. – You are very beautiful. – The older woman said again, slower this time, getting up and sitting on the edge of the bed.

– Thank you. – Smiling slightly, Milena replied.

"In spite of your age, you are beautiful too," Milena thought, but did not say anything.

The older woman was indeed strikingly beautiful. Through her wrinkled face, it was not difficult to see her true features, unaffected by age. Blue eyes in which all her past life had swum, as if in a pool.

– Are you married? – The woman asked suddenly, looking at Milena.

Milena looked at her and shook her head. The woman sighed and looked away.

– Your eyes are dull. They're very kind, good, but there's something missing. – She continued to speak, staring into space. – It hurts me to see such a pretty young girl unhappy.

Milena wanted to object, but stopped herself in time. The woman, oblivious to the young lady's confusion, continued.

– Life is an interesting thing. It defies logic. It plays with us all the time. It lifts us up or down, or, having lifted us up, forgets to catch us. We meet reality. And it's hard. And it hurts. I'm on the verge of death, ready to say goodbye to it. But... I still can't understand her. Maybe you can. I don't know. There are some questions better left unanswered. You get lost in the labyrinth of the unanswerable.

I was 18 when I met him. I was a beautiful, carefree girl, enjoying every moment without realising it. How I longed every day to go back there. At that time, life and I had not yet met. When I met him, something boiled in my stomach, my heart jumped. I was afraid. I ran home through the meadows and hid in my little room. I was lucky. My parents weren't home, otherwise I would have had to answer all their questions.

He was a stranger to me. I'd never seen him in our village. I knew everyone there. You must smile at the stupidity of an 18–year– old girl. Nowadays girls are much smarter, stronger, more focused. It was a different time, different morals, a different life.

The second time I met him was when my mother sent me to the neighbour's house to get coal. He was talking to the neighbour's boy. Tall, slim, with light skin, not typical of a country boy, brown eyes, a stern, penetrating look. A short– sleeved T– shirt revealed strong but not very muscular arms, close– cropped hair just visible at the temples – his head was covered by a grey cap. Trousers pulled up at the knees covered his long legs. Strangely, he was barefoot. Seventy years have passed, but his face is etched in my mind. And I know that when I close my eyes for the last time, it will be his face in front of me.

Milena listened in silence, looking at the older woman. With each word, a picture formed in Milena's mind.

– I won't bore you. – The woman continued, still staring into space. – When I saw him, my heart jumped again. I wanted to turn around and go home, but the neighbour's boyfriend noticed me and called out. "Anna, hi."

Milena smiled as she finally recognised the name of her interlocutor.

– I stood there, pinned to the floor. I couldn't move. He looked at me with his penetrating gaze. I gave up. My legs and arms were getting weaker. I dropped the bag in which I wanted to put the money. He smiled, put his hands in his pockets and kept looking at me. Intently. I was so embarrassed. "Anna, can I help you?" Gurgen called me again. "No." I finally answered and started walking as hard as I could to the door of the house where Gurgen and the stranger were standing.

Vigen, that was his name, turned out to be a man from the north, where he and his parents had lived for a long time. They had moved to Armenia and came to our village on holiday to look after my grandmother. He was six years my senior. He managed to get a higher education that I could only dream of. I don't know what to call my feelings for him. I worshipped him, idolised him, breathed only him. He was everything to an ordinary country girl. Believe me, I meant the same to him.

We spent all summer together. Running away from home, away from prying eyes. With him I discovered a new world, a new me. Thanks to him, I entered the Pedagogical University that autumn and moved to Yerevan. Our relationship became stronger, more serious, more meaningful. He became my incentive to study. I was the first in my class.

Day after day, I waited for him to propose. And that day came. It was probably the best and worst day of my life. I mean, after all these years, it still gets me choked up.

You're probably wondering why. What happened? His father was killed in the north. He was travelling there on business when his family got the sad news. Vigen and his family left. My parents wouldn't let me go with them. According to the customs of the villagers, an unmarried girl could not leave with her lover.

I don't want to tell you how difficult it was for me. After all, we had spent three wonderful years together. Day after day, I waited to hear from him. I waited for him to come and for us to get married. A month passed, six months, six months, a year, two years. I left the institute in a hurry. I never got the red diploma I wanted. The city was empty for me. I returned to the village. I started to work as a primary school teacher. A year later, when I was twenty–four, my parents married me to a businessman from the city who came to our village from time to time to work. I didn't love him, of course, but over the years I grew fond of him. We lived together for 63 years. We had two daughters and a son. My husband died last year. I decided to move into a nursing home so that I wouldn't be a burden on my children. After all, it will soon be my turn.

Anna finally looked at Milena with her blue eyes. Milena was trembling, clear drops dripping from her eyes. Anna ran her hand down Milena's cheek, wiping away her tears.

– I'm sorry, my little girl. I didn't mean to make you sad.

– No, not at all. It's all right. It's you who forgive me. – Milena said, getting up from her seat. – I had to come and talk to you, to cheer you up. But because of me you had to remember everything again and get sad.

Anna didn't answer. There was a knock at the door.

– Excuse me, may I?

It was Ani.

When she didn't get an answer, she stopped at the door.

– Sorry to disturb you, but Milena, we have to go. – Yes, of course.

– Yes, of course. I'll be right back. – Milena said.

– Yes, of course. – Ani said and disappeared behind the door.

Milena came to Anna, leaned over and hugged her tightly without asking permission. Anna hugged Milena too and whispered.

– Life is too short to make mistakes and spend it with the wrong person.

Milena smiled through her tears. She said goodbye to Anna and followed Ani out the door.

On her way out she wrote a note.

"I'm sorry. I love you. We need to talk."

In Republic Square, crowds of people, most of them tourists, gathered around the singing fountains. At exactly nine o'clock in the evening, music was played and the jets of water, accompanied by multi– coloured spotlights, swirled to the rhythm of the music. The spectacle was beautiful, soothing and emotional at the same time.

The song played was Adiemus from the film Avatar.

She stood to the right of the Fantans. Her arms crossed over her chest, she held her breath as she watched the chaotic dance of the water jets. Her body was covered with millions of goose bumps. She opened her mouth periodically to inhale the fresh, damp, cool air. Her eyes didn't blink. They just burned with a strange fire. Something was happening inside. Emotions were running high.

Her heart was racing, the rhythm of it giving her body goose bumps, and she hugged her shoulders tighter and tighter, trying to keep the shivers at bay.

But the shaking reached its limit when she felt a familiar breath at the back of her neck. And the scent of his favourite perfume filled her nostrils, despite the damp air.

Silently, he stepped close to her. He took her in his arms and rested his chin on her shoulder. Milena closed her eyes. Her limbs felt pleasantly weak. Where he touched her, even through her clothes, her body burned. Her heart was pumping blood to the rhythm of the music, filling her with a pleasant warmth.

Genuine, incomparable happiness flowed through her body. With her eyes closed, Milena continued to savour the moment, afraid to miss even a little of it.

– Don't let me go. Never. Do you hear me? – Milena whispered suddenly, turning her head to look at Gor with an excited, passionate gaze. – I can't go on without you. Hold me tight. And don't let go. Never.

He hugged her tighter and kissed her on the top of her head.

The songs changed from one to another. The fountains swirled in a chaotic dance. People came and went. The clock on the government building continued its hard, uninterrupted work. The day was drawing to a close. Only one couple could not get enough of each other and stayed in a tight embrace for more than an hour.

"Hey, Vlad. How are you? I'm sorry I haven't called you back the last two days. I just can't talk to you. I can't because I feel so guilty about you.

I hope you'll understand, not judge, and forgive me.

I haven't been honest with you. The only reason I went to Moscow was to forget someone. I thought the distance would help. I met you by chance. You're unique. Honestly. I had a wonderful time with you. And I liked you. But...

I can't explain how I feel. But by choosing you, I'm hurting both of us. It's not right.

When I came to Yerevan and saw Gor again, I realised that I still loved him and that I would never be able to love anyone like that again.

Forgive me for giving you false hope. I hope you will find someone in your life who truly deserves the love of the perfect man you are.

Goodbye Vlad."

Sent.

Chapter 13

August 2016

"Hi Astine.

I've never noticed leaf– fall in August. Yellow crumpled leaves filled the whole city. It's weird, isn't it? No, it's not weird. The summer was too hot. It's the hottest I've ever been in Armenia in my entire life.

The green leaves couldn't stand the hot sun. Even nature was defeated by an overdose of heat. And what to speak about people? We are just like leaves that dislike both cold and overheating."

Milena hadn't expected this turn of events at all. Being Aren's sister and Ani's close friend, she had no idea that during the two years of Aren's service, she and Ani had been in contact.

So, when the young ones announced that they were going to get married, not only the parents of both parties but also Milena was shocked but pleasantly surprised. During so many years of friendship between the children, the parents managed not only to get acquainted, but also gained warm friendships.

The engagement took place at Anya's parents' house in a small circle of relatives. Both families were enthusiastically preparing for the upcoming wedding, which was scheduled for the twentieth of August.

Armenia is beautiful. There are so many interesting, mysterious and fascinating things in it. For tourists it is a wonderland where you can be inspired by every stone. And most of them do their best to visit maximum places and enjoy the beauty of all Armenia in minimum time. But unfortunately, even the locals never get to know and discover all the charms of their country.

Before the upcoming wedding, the young people decided to go to Arkaz Monastery or as it is commonly called Surb Khach Church.

Surb Khach Church is located in Vayots Dzor province, 8 km east of Vernashen village, in the valley of Malishka river, on the site of Arkazn settlement, which in ancient times was one of the famous settlements in Vayots Dzor province of Syunik region of Greater Armenia and is mentioned in historical documents since the 8th century.

The church was fully reconstructed in 2011.

The church of Surb Khach is a truly holy place. People from all parts of the country go there with a spark of hope and return with a flame in their souls. People believe in the undeniable power of this place. Many claims that their prayers have been heard within the cold walls of the monastery, and more than once.

Milena was preparing with particular excitement and love for the upcoming wedding of her brother and best friend. Her maturing relationship with Gor inspired her with inexhaustible energy. A sincere smile returned to the sweet face of the golden– haired beauty. Her brown eyes sparkled.

"I look forward to this day with heart palpitations. It's a shame you won't be able to make it. Can you imagine if the baby girl is born on your wedding day? That would be awesome.

Gor and I will be together at the wedding. Can you imagine? I can't believe we made it through this whole nightmare. But now, thank God, things are better than ever. My parents didn't approve of my decision to invite him. They still can't forgive him for my pain. That's weird. I don't remember it at all. All the bad stuff fades away. Is it a defence function of my body? I don't know. Whatever it is, it's working perfectly.

The maid of honour will be Ani's younger sister Inna. And as best man, Aren chose a friend from the army, with whom he served two years and with whom he went through the war.

That's it, darling. I'm off to get ready. I have a fitting today. I'll send a photo. I hope you like my blue silk dress. You take care of yourself. Be careful, my girl.

Kisses and hugs."

In recent years, Armenian weddings have been notable for their fusion of Armenian traditions and customs with modern European creativity. They are celebrated without national bias and without pressure from both close and distant relatives and parents, as the tradition, which came to us from distant ancestors, sometimes leads to curious situations.

Nowadays, every Armenian couple who have decided to become husband and wife decide for themselves what customs will be at their celebration. And it is right. No one wants to remember the most important day of their lives with shivers and tears, regretting the fact that they followed the traditions and did not act according to the dictates of their heart.

Regardless of everything, an Armenian wedding is a bright, colourful and memorable event.

"Astine, my dear. "Congratulations on the birth of your baby girl. My Nelly. I can't wait to see her and hold her in my arms. I knew she'd be born on Anya and Aren's wedding day. When you get a chance, please send me a picture of our baby girl.

I'm sending you some pictures from the wedding right now. You have no idea what an exciting and unforgettable day it was.

Our newlyweds just left a couple of hours ago for their honeymoon. Yes, yes. To the Maldives. Just like Ani dreamed of.

Astine, I'm so happy, I can't sit still. My heart is jumping up and down, and I'm jumping up and down with it. I haven't had such positive emotions and experiences in a long time. Everything is beautiful. Everyone around me is happy.

The gore at the wedding was beautiful. Relatives and friends could not take their eyes off us. We received a lot of compliments. We did more than one dance. He – in a strict black suit, and I – in my Cinderella dress, drowning in his arms.

Hopefully, in time, his parents will forgive him. Although they didn't give away their confusion at the wedding. They were very nice to him. And it's all for me. They're the best.

I hope, Astine, that Gor and I are getting married soon. We haven't broached the subject yet. I don't want to rush it either. It'll be different this time. All in good time. I just want to enjoy our love every day.

Astine, watch yourself. Say hi to Armen. Answer when it's convenient for you. Right now all your attention should be on a little miracle named Nelly."

Chapter 14

September, 2016

The message Milena received was from some MM. No pictures, no personal details of any kind. It was a long message. At first glance, Milena thought it was just another ad, but when she happened to notice a painfully familiar name in the line, her trembling fingers scrolled down the screen to the beginning of the text.

With each line, with each word, Milena's heart tightened. Her mouth went dry. Consciousness blurred. The pain was searing.

"Hello, Milena. You must have been surprised to get this message from a stranger. To be honest, I don't know if you know I exist. But judging by what's been going on in your life these past few months, you can at least guess.

My name is Nina.

And? That name sounds familiar. I think it does. There's no way someone who knows Gor wouldn't have mentioned it. And, of course, the sad story behind it.

You're wondering how I know about you, why I'm writing about you. I don't think you're going to like my answer. Believe me, I have nothing against you. I have my own life with my own quirks. And frankly, I don't care how you live yours.

But there's something you need to know. And I should be the one to tell you, since Gor won't. It's fair to both of us. I won't try your patience. You're already on your toes, asking a million questions.

Gor and I have a son, Milena. You don't believe me? That's to be expected. But it's the truth. It's the truth.

You ask when? How? How did this happen? You're entitled to wonder. Just a few more lines and you'll find out.

Gor left the army before he was supposed to. I had already met someone else. Someone with whom I'd learnt what true love and passion were. There was nothing like Gor. I'd already made up my mind, rehearsed the conversation several times in my head. But as soon as we met, all my thoughts and my carefully crafted monologue disappeared. I slept with Gor. The night was unforgettable, to be honest. Especially for Gor. But even spending the night with my ex– fiancé didn't make me change my mind and stay. While he slept, I packed up, left the ring next to his watch on the bedside table and ran away for what I thought was forever.

I got pregnant. My husband was happy. Nine months later we had a boy, Karen. His eyes were dark from birth. My husband was surprised because we are both green– eyed, although his father and grandfather are dark– eyed. I guessed, but deep down I didn't want to accept the truth. But it all lasted until I decided to have a second child. After careful and unsuccessful attempts, it turned out that my husband was infertile. And that's when everything came to a head. The truth came out. I told my husband everything. To my surprise, he didn't leave me. He loves me and my son very much.

How did Gor find out? Does he even know? I'll be honest with you. If it was up to me, I wouldn't have let it happen. I didn't want to ruin my relationship with my husband, for which I had to pay too high a price. I dropped out of school. My family, my relatives, my friends all turned their backs on me.

You probably think I'm stupid, too stupid. But I'm not. No one has the right to judge me. I'm really happy now.

One day I was walking with Karen in the park, holding his hand tightly. He was already four years old. The month of December last year. But despite the winter, the weather was perfect. Suddenly, out of nowhere, Gor appeared in front of me. He was surprised, depressed. I can't even describe the feelings and emotions that were on his face. I was, frankly, terrified. I took my son in my arms and held him tightly to my chest.

As luck would have it, living in the same city, we never even happened to meet after we broke up. We hadn't seen each other for too long. But when I saw the pain in his eyes, I felt remorse for the first time since the day we broke up. He owed that pain to me. I knew it. He looked back and forth at me, then at the boy. The surprise was growing. The same coal– black eyes, the same piercing expression. He didn't need any more words. One look at the boy was enough for him to realise it all for himself.

It was the end of March, you had a gig at the club that day. I saw the poster. I knew Gor was going to be there. But that afternoon my son fell off a swing in the playground and hurt his arm and we had to take him to the hospital. We were only treated for a bad bruise, so the child was discharged a few hours later. During all this time Gor never left the hospital.

Things got more difficult from there, both for me and for him. He did everything he could to see the baby, to see me. And I did everything possible and impossible to make sure my husband didn't suspect a thing.

I swear this is not how I imagined our meeting. Knowing Gor's temperament, I thought he'd kill me when we met. But to my great surprise, it turned out to be quite the opposite.

I know it will hurt you terribly to hear this, but Gor tried to rebuild our relationship again, despite all the agony and suffering he went through because of me. Despite the fact that I was married.

It's been a long time since we met, and he still calls me and sees my son and me.

Milena, there's something I need to tell you. I know I have no right to say it, but I can't keep quiet. And so I'm punishing myself for not writing to you sooner. It's just that I've weighed the pros and cons many times.

The day we first met, he was holding a jewellery box. He quickly hid it in the inside pocket of his jacket, but I could still see it. When I asked him about it, he was silent for a long time, but soon he told me about you. Not in detail, of course. But that was enough for me. I know him very well. He bought you a ring, he was going to propose. But that was the day he met me and my son.

I hate myself for that. I mean, afterwards, he said he couldn't commit to another woman knowing he had a son growing up. Stupid, I know.

Believe me, please, I begged him more than once. But he was adamant. And then he wouldn't even let me talk about you. And when I asked him if he loved you, he was silent, he looked into my eyes with his penetrating gaze. And in that moment, green and black merged again.

I don't know how my letter will affect you and your relationship, but at least know that people don't change. He who betrayed once will strike again. The one who abandoned – will abandon the second time. The one who turned his back without a second thought – will turn his back at the next opportune moment. People do not change. Only their attitudes change and at their discretion. Know how to let go of those who have neglected you. Know how to forgive, but with closed arms. Forgive and let go. Forever.

I tell you this from my own experience. From my own life.

I didn't mean to hurt you or to hurt you. I just didn't want you to be deceived.

My husband and I have decided to leave. We'll probably go to Moscow. He's been offered a job there. A decent one. I didn't want to leave. But after meeting Gor, I think it's the best decision. Otherwise, I risk losing the only thing I value in my life. After all, I lost everything else a long time ago.

I hope that with my departure, your relationship with Gor will resume and come to its logical happy conclusion.

I don't know you. But honestly, I don't want to be the cause of your pain.

I wish you the best of luck. Goodbye."

Her arms and legs went weak. Milena dropped the phone. Sat on the edge of the couch. She didn't move for a long time, staring at one point and breathing occasionally. A cold veil enveloped her entire body. Her heart beat sporadically. With each beat a trickle of warmth flowed through her body, which was immediately replaced by coldness and emptiness.

How long Milena sat like that, she can't remember. But she woke up in her bed in the morning. The room was lit by the autumn sun, and there was a pleasant coolness. Milena slowly got out of bed, looked out of the window and breathed in the air she lacked.

A normal working day. Hot coffee with a croissant, a blue dress with short sleeves, a car, some strangely empty roads, a clinic, a white coat, patients. And it was as if nothing had changed.

She continued to live her usual life: smiling, laughing, going to work, seeing patients, meeting with friends, going to rehearsals.

As difficult as it was, Milena ignored Gor's calls and messages. He was perplexed. He didn't understand what was going on. But she didn't react. After work, she noticed his car outside the clinic more than once. But she left the building only when he, tired of waiting, finally drove away.

Milena didn't manage to hide from Gor for long. He caught her by surprise at her car. There was no way she could avoid the encounter.

Her heart clenched in her chest as soon as she saw him. Her breathing quickened. But she tried her best to hide the sensational emotion.

– Hi.

– Hi, Gor.

He came up for a kiss. She turned her head. He touched her temple with his lips. But that touch was enough to make them both shivers.

– Don't you have anything to say to me?

Milena turned her head in bewilderment, looking at him. He continued.

– Why are you avoiding me?

– I'm not. I have no reason to avoid you. – She said, averting her gaze.

– I wouldn't say that. I haven't been able to contact you in over a week. You don't answer calls or texts, you don't leave the clinic.

– I've got a lot of work to do. That's all. – Milena replied, continuing to stare at nothing.

– Look at me when I'm talking to you. – said Gor, taking Milena by the chin and turning her head towards him.

She looked into his black favourite eyes. Milena had so many words piling up, so many emotions that she wanted to spill out, to say everything to his face. But she remained silent. She still couldn't say the words that were important to her.

He stared at her in silence. She did not know what was going on in his soul, in his head. She thought she knew him in detail, but it turned out she didn't know this guy at all.

Their eyes cried out, but they both stood quietly, not daring to speak.

– Milena, I came to say goodbye.

Milena looked up at him with an unsurprised, hurt look. Gor leaned against her car, crossed his arms on his chest and continued.

– I was offered a job in Moscow. In one of the best private hospitals. I couldn't refuse. It's a big opportunity. I don't know when I'll be able to come. I don't know if I'll ever get there. I didn't think it would turn out like this.

Milena smiled. It's funny to hear lies when you know the truth. Yes, it is. But Milena couldn't give herself away in any way by admitting that she knew the truth about his departure. She only said.

– "Of course. I understand. You really shouldn't miss this chance. It's a once– in– a– lifetime opportunity.

Gor looked at her in surprise.

– "I'm sorry, my girl. I didn't mean to hurt you. I don't know if I'm doing the right thing. But I have to. I have no other choice.

Milena only nodded. Gor continued.

– I'll never forget you, Milena. Your image, your eyes, your smile, your scent will haunt me all my life, without the most important thing of all: you. But I don't want to keep you either. I don't want to give you false hope. I don't want," he paused for a moment, took a sip of saliva, and finally said, "for you to wait for me.

Milena approached him calmly, feeling nothing, understanding nothing, realising nothing. She ran her hand over his unshaven, prickly cheek. Looked into his black favourite dear eyes.

– I can't imagine my life without you, I can't imagine a night without the memories of a day with you. – She paused for a moment. But with a special serenity she continued. – Go away, Gor. Go after your dream. I won't hold you back. I'm letting you go.

He hugged her tightly. She surrendered.

– I love you. I love you too much, Gor. And the only thing I want is for you to be happy. I agree to an eternal distance between us, I agree to never see you again, to leave us in the past, to go on living without knowing love, only knowing that you have found peace and happiness.

Lowering her down, he looked into her eyes again. Her eyes were screaming. But she remained calm.

– Milena, I...

– Don't say any more, Gor, please. It's better this way. Just go away quietly. I'll be all right. I promise.

And without another word, Milena walked over to Gor, closed her eyes, kissed him on the left cheek, took a last deep breath of his scent, opened her eyes, but without looking at him again, walked to the car. Without looking back, she drove off, leaving only a small cloud of smoke behind.

"And time passed, Astine. The days passed one after the other. But as it turned out, I simply didn't understand, didn't want to understand what had really happened. My mind had covered me with a kind of defensive shell to prevent me from suffering, to protect me from reality. But the shell didn't last long.

One day I was late for work. Everyone had left. I was alone, looking at patient profiles. Just like that, not thinking, not reading, just flicking through. The laptop was on. Music was playing. Another song. To be honest, I wasn't even listening. Until it was the one that had accompanied him and me more than once.

Suddenly I stopped. I put the forms down on the table. It was like an electric shock. It was like waking up. I opened my eyes and took a deep breath.

I sat down on the cold floor and leaned against the wall. And that's when I sobbed for the first time. I sobbed at the top of my lungs. As hard as I could. The accumulated pain coursed through my body like poison circulating in my blood. Lying on the cold floor, I couldn't move. Everything inside me froze. Everything inside collapsed. The shell exploded. Only then did I realise the truth of what had happened.

It hurt too much. I won't lie.

Which of us was responsible? Nina, Gor, me? No one, Astine. We all just wanted to be happy. And in the end, all three of us are unhappy. Nina told me she'd found happiness. But I don't believe it. No matter how much she loves her husband and son, deep down she'll always miss everything she lost – her parents, her friends, her unfinished university.

Gor... Every time I think of him, my heart breaks. I swear, if I knew he would be truly happy away from me, I would have let him go in the first place. He's so close and yet so far away from them, from Nina and her son. She will never leave her husband, never accept Gor and never tell her son about him. Gor knows all this very well, of course. But... I don't blame him. I understand him. It's his choice. It's his destiny.

But what about me? What about me?

I couldn't believe it, or rather I didn't want to believe it. Everything that had happened between us had been a waste, a lie, one big deception, a game of my sick, sentimental imagination.

I realised one thing. First love is never forgotten. It fades, but it never completely disappears. Nina was and always will be Gor's one and only love. And that is undeniable. Because that's what he is to me.

How stupid I was, how naive, how empty. And he kept telling me that there was no future for us. And I didn't believe it. My faith was filled only by his, as it seemed to me, sincere kisses and caresses. My hope never faded.

Now I had the answers to all the questions, Astine, that I had been asking myself and you all this time. He found them in December. That's when everything changed for us.

I lost the love I had played with myself. The world my imagination had created was destroyed. All that was left was rubble, just shards of my soul, my body and my broken heart.

I waited for a fairy tale, I waited for a miracle. I won't lie. With him gone, I hoped to finally breathe again. I hoped to wake up one morning with a different thought that wasn't about him.

But...

Not a day went by that I didn't think about him. Every morning, every night, I waited to hear from him. I'd wake up in the middle of the night and stare at my smartphone, waiting for something with his name on it. But it was all in vain. He was silent. He never spoke. He never called or texted a word. I waited for him to come and for me to receive him. I'd seen too many happy endings. And now my happy ending wouldn't let me rest. I let him go. At least that's what I thought. I hoped.

But my heart, my bloody heart, held on to him as tight as it could.

I know you knew or found out in time. I don't know and I don't want to know the reason why you kept quiet. I hope it is valid and worthwhile.

I still wonder how I managed to survive all this. I'm not strong enough.

Did he really love me? I don't know. I don't think I'll ever know the answer.

When I look back, I go back to our past with him, where I left the best and happiest days of my life.

Will I ever be happy again? I don't know.

I'm not smiling, Astine. I haven't smiled for a long time. Everything has gone black. My world is black and white now. No one can see my pain. No one ever will. It lurks deep inside of me where no one can get in forever.

I miss you so much. I want to lie down, put my head on your lap and just be quiet.

The only thing that makes me feel better is time. I know it won't let me down. Because when I think of what used to torment me, I smile now. And maybe after some time has passed, I'll smile again, remembering it all.

Love, kiss, miss. No matter what."

Sent.

Epilogue

Yerevan, 2017, early April

Spring came late this year. But the spring sun and warmth did not leave Armenians languishing for long. The winter was hard. The inhabitants of the capital had not experienced such cold since ancient times. After winter frosts, endless snow, fog and clouds, the warm April sun was invaluable as never before.

Milena managed to pass her final exams and proudly held her head high as she completed her residency, the final stage of her medical training. She got a job in a dental clinic near the medical university on Abovyan Street. She didn't complain about the number of patients. She worked with great enthusiasm. Almost everyone was happy.

In May, Karina planned a European tour. Milena looked forward to the trip with childlike excitement.

St Anna's Church at the crossroads of Abovyan and Sayat–Nova streets. Sunshine, a light April breeze.

"Hello. How long has it been since I've been here? I'm sorry. I was just offended. I couldn't understand why all the pain. It's taken me a while to realise and understand. It's a bit hard for me.

I've suffered. Honestly. But I didn't know it, and thanks to you I don't know real suffering. After the war I realised that it was boundless.

Today I just came to talk. To say a few words and leave quietly. I didn't come to ask you or thank you or anything like that. I just came to talk and to say that I have finally taken off my old dress and now my frame is free. My caterpillar today will become a butterfly who will live each day as her last. Appreciating everything she has. Will pursue everything she longs for. But will also enjoy her life to the full.

I don't know how long my butterfly will fly, but I do know that her flight will be remembered for a long time.

Goodbye and farewell.

Milena walked slowly towards the door. She prepared to make an effort to open it, because it was always difficult to open, but to her surprise, Milena managed it easily.

Suddenly a tall, handsome man in his thirties appeared in front of her. He was wearing an austere dark blue suit. There was no tie. The top buttons of his snow– white shirt were undone. Thanks to him, the door gave way easily.

Milena looked up in confusion and met the astonished gaze of black eyes that seemed very familiar to her.

He had never entered the church. After holding the door, he stepped aside and let Milena out.

– Hello. – He said suddenly. – Don't you recognise me?

– Hello. – Milena replied in surprise. – No, to be honest. Do we know each other?

– Not personally, but we met at your parents' office. Milena, right?

– Yes. – Right. And you?

– I am Armen. Nice to meet you. – He said, holding out his hand.

– Mutually. – Milena replied, looking at the outstretched

hand of her new acquaintance. After a moment's hesitation, she extended hers.

Armen gently squeezed her fragile palm. Milena looked down at her hands again. Then she slowly looked up at Armen. He smiled sweetly.

– I'm sorry, I don't remember you.

– That's OK, it happens.

– Are you a client of hers? – Milena asked, slightly interested.

– No. – I'm a lawyer too. I have an important case with your parents. So, I will be a regular guest in their office in the near future. – said the young man, his coal– black eyes still flashing.

– I see. You're lucky. You know what you're doing.

– I know. That's why I agreed to work with you right away.

– That's great.

– Yes. – It is.

– Well, I'm gonna go. It was nice to meet you. – Milena knew she had to go, but some inexplicable force held her back.

– Yes, of course. I won't keep you. I hope we'll meet again soon. – Armen said with a special tone.

– Of course. The meeting is inevitable. – Milena replied, surprised at herself.

Turning her back on her new acquaintance, Milena walked towards Abovyan Street with a special smile.

– Bye, Milena. – Armen called after her.

She just turned her head slightly, smiled and continued on her way without saying a word.

It was her first smile in six months.

One day she was handed a piece of paper with the words: "What do you think happiness is?"

She smiled slightly. Picked up a pen. And started writing.

PRIZE BY HERTFORDSHIRE PRESS
FOR THE BEST WORK IN THE PROSE CATEGORY

Over the past twelve years, Hertfordshire Press has had the privilege of supporting talented authors from Eurasian countries, with the aim of promoting its unique culture. We are grateful to the annual grant for the winner in the Prose category of the Open Eurasia literary contest (also known as OEBF*) for enabling more than ten authors to be published in London and to become significant figures in their home countries.

The contest, which began with 120 participants in 2012, has grown to include 1,400 participants each year, making the OEBF award one of the oldest, most significant, and highly regarded literary awards in Eurasia. We are pleased to say that the total prize pool over the years has reached $70,000. We are delighted to report that we are experiencing growth, development and progress. We are grateful to have had the opportunity to engage with over 14,000 individuals from 85 countries across the globe over the past 12 years. We were delighted to welcome over 3,000 guests from 25 countries to our festivals and forums in Bishkek, Almaty, London, Oxford, Cambridge, Bangkok, Stockholm, Brussels and elsewhere. We would be delighted to welcome our esteemed friends, both old and new, to join us.

Hertfordshire Press (UK) is a distinctive British publishing house that strives to bridge the gap between English-speaking readers and Eurasia through the publication of books, magazines, and guidebooks by authors from the region. We are happy to be able to offer authors the opportunity to have their work published in 12 different languages. We are pleased to be able to offer our books in both hard copy and electronic versions.

Since 2002, the publishing house has been focusing on the publication of modern fiction and popular scientific literature by Eurasian authors, as well as the republication of works from previous years which are not currently available in English. We are proud to share that our catalogue contains over 250 works by authors from 17 countries, with a total print run of over 1,000,000 copies.

*The Open Eurasian Literature Festival & Book Forum (OEBF) is a distinctive annual event that plays a unique role in promoting Eurasian literature on an international scale. As a cultural bridge between East and West, it offers a valuable platform for authors and artists to engage in dialogue about their work, share experiences and connect with like-minded individuals from diverse countries, fostering potential collaborations.

*Please don't hesitate to contact us at
publisher@ocamagazine.com or visit our website at
www.eng.awardslondon.com
or www.eurasiancreativeguild.uk.*